The elegant stranger grasped Bob's arm. "Come along now."

Bob tried to pull back, but the man's grip was like steel. The young Investigator shouted. Then he threw himself at the water cooler and hung on, yelling.

"Now see here, son," said the stranger.

The store manager appeared. "Trouble?" he said.

"Not really," said the stranger. "My boy's been up to—"

"Kidnapper!" croaked Bob. "Crook! Get the cops, mister! This guy isn't my dad. I never saw him before in my life!"

The Mystery
of the
Trail of Terror

by
M. V. Carey

based on characters created by Robert Arthur

BULLSEYE BOOKS
ALFRED A. KNOPF • NEW YORK

Contents

A Word from Hector Sebastian

It's my pleasure to introduce you to The Three Investigators. If you've already met these unusual detectives, turn to Chapter 1 right away. If not, let me do the honors.

We begin with Jupiter Jones, who is the leader of the group. He is smarter than the average boy, and he has read more and remembered more than most people I know. He also can take a few facts and work with them to come to some amazing conclusions.

Pete Crenshaw is the most athletic of The Three Investigators, and he's also cheerful, loyal, and easygoing. He feels that Jupe can sometimes think up stunts that are a little too dangerous, and he may not be the only one who has this opinion.

Bob Andrews is quiet and less flamboyant, and he is in charge of records and research for the group. That doesn't mean he sits back and lets the others do their daring deeds alone. Bob is as brave as his colleagues.

As for me, I'm a retired detective and have turned my hand to writing mystery novels. I came to know The Three Investigators through a scar-faced beggar, but that's another story. Suffice it to say that I send whatever mysteries I hear about their way and introduce their cases.

This mystery is one that The Three Investigators found themselves. In it, the boys leave their home in Rocky Beach, California, and set out on a vacation trip across the United States. The vacation becomes a flight from terror when they are followed by an unshakable menace that always remains just out of reach.

Curious? Who wouldn't be? Then turn to Chapter 1 and start the adventure!

HECTOR SEBASTIAN

The Mystery
of the
Trail of Terror

1

A Walking Disaster

The kitchen door banged open. Then it slammed shut. Mrs. Crenshaw stormed into the kitchen. Her lips were set and her cheeks were flushed.

"I'll murder the old geezer!" she announced. "He's a walking disaster! I'll shoot him, and no jury will ever convict me!"

She glared at her son, Pete, and then at his friends Jupiter Jones and Bob Andrews.

"Drenched!" said Mrs. Crenshaw. "Every member of the Ladies Guild—just drenched! I met Mrs. Harrison at the market and she told me."

"Oh," said Pete. "It's Grandpa again!"

"Who else would it be?" demanded his mother. "You know what he did this time? Out of the goodness of his heart he donated a new sprinkler system for the church hall. He installed it himself, with a new supersensitive, smoke-activated gizmo as a trigger for the system. An invention of his, of course. Yesterday the ladies were having a fashion show and the pastor wandered in and was careless enough to light a cigarette!"

Pete tried not to smile, but he couldn't help himself.

"It's not funny!" snapped Mrs. Crenshaw. But then she relented. The corners of her mouth turned up and she smiled. The boys started chuckling and soon all of them—Mrs. Crenshaw included—were roaring with laughter.

"I guess he did strike a blow for clean air," she admitted.

She sat down at the kitchen table, wiping her eyes, and the boys stayed where they were, leaning against the counters and eating cookies.

"Even before he retired, my father wasn't like other people," said Mrs. Crenshaw. "Once he built a house with a roof that folded back like a convertible car. Crazy! Nobody would live in it. It leaked!"

"Mr. Peck does have some original ideas," said Jupe carefully.

Mrs. Crenshaw grimaced. "The fashion show yesterday morning must have been original beyond words."

"Come on, Mom, Grandpa will make good on it, won't he?" said Pete. "He always does."

"That's why we were never rich," said Mrs. Crenshaw. "Someday he'll wind up in prison with his crazy schemes. Not everything gets fixed with money."

That was true. Not long before, a crew from the Rocky Beach Parks Department had attempted to remove a diseased elm tree that grew in front of Mr. Peck's house. Determined to protect his property, the old gentleman had come dashing out with a baseball bat and had driven the tree men back to their truck. Two of Police Chief Reynolds' men had appeared and tried to reason with Mr. Peck. When that failed, they had taken him to jail in handcuffs. Mrs. Crenshaw had had to post bond for him, and then had to insist that he hire a lawyer. The charge had eventually been reduced from assault with a deadly weapon to disorderly conduct, and Mr. Peck had paid a fine and listened to a warning. The tree men had not ventured back to remove the tree; it remained as a monument to Mr. Peck's temper and his stubborn will.

"And now he wants to go to New York," said Mrs. Crenshaw.

Pete was stunned. "To live?" he asked. "Hey, he wouldn't really move away, would he?"

"No. He's invented something that's so important he won't even talk about it, and he wants to present it to the proper people. Apparently they're in New York. Pop says the telephone won't do and the mail won't do. He has to go in person."

"Okay," said Pete. "What's wrong with that?"

"Suppose the people don't want to see him in person? Suppose they tell him to go home and write a letter? He'll force his way in!"

"Mom, you're exaggerating."

"I am not. I know my father. He doesn't take no for an answer. And if the people he wants to see don't like his idea, he'll lose his temper and accuse them of being morons."

"Mom, really—"

"Believe me, I know him!" Mrs. Crenshaw insisted. "He'll threaten and they'll call the cops. It will be like the time he improved the solar water heater so much that the thing actually boiled water. Or the time that new room humidifier—"

"That one worked!" Pete pointed out.

"It did indeed. Only somebody had invented it before Pop got around to it, and Pop swore they'd stolen it from him. If you could please tell me how a guy who lives in Dubuque, Iowa, could swipe an invention from a guy in Rocky Beach, California, I would be grateful!"

Pete was silent.

Jupiter and Bob exchanged a quizzical look.

"Besides Pop just *being* in New York, which is sure to make trouble, there's the trip," said Mrs. Crenshaw.

"Mom, Grandpa's been on planes before. We'll take him to the airport and—"

"He's driving," said Mrs. Crenshaw. "All the way. Across the whole wide country. He's going through Montana. He says he's never seen Montana, and he hasn't been to Oregon or Washington either, and he doesn't want to miss anything. He says he does some of his best creative thinking when he's driving. Maybe that explains why he's gotten so many speeding tickets."

Pete grinned. "Mom, if you're so worried, why don't you go with Grandpa? Dad and I will be okay, and the trip would be fun—"

"It would not be fun," declared Mrs. Crenshaw. "Not for me. Not with Pop. You know we can't be together for ten seconds without a fight. If you think driving all across the country with him would be such a lark, you can go."

Pete's eyes widened. "You mean it? Boy, would that be a blast!"

"Would it?" challenged his mother. "Could you keep him out of trouble? See to it that he doesn't get arrested and doesn't attack anyone?"

"Hey, Mom, sure. I mean, I'll give it my best try, but—"

"But you don't think you can do it, do you?" said his mother. "Okay. He's always been—"

Suddenly she stopped and stared at Jupiter. The chunky boy was solemnly gobbling up a chocolate cookie. But though his mouth was active, his eyes looked as if he were daydreaming. It was a look that did not mislead Mrs. Crenshaw. Jupe, as his friends called him, was the leader of The Three Investigators. Mrs. Crenshaw knew that Jupe could pay close attention to everything that went on around him, even when he appeared drowsy and absent-minded. She also knew that Jupe had an almost perfect memory. If she asked him, he could probably repeat the conversation she had just had, word for word.

Mrs. Crenshaw sometimes felt intimidated by Jupe. He was so self-possessed. It didn't seem natural in one who was so young. But now Jupe seemed like the answer to her prayer.

"I would like to retain The Three Investigators," said Mrs. Crenshaw suddenly.

The Three Investigators was a junior detective agency that the three boys had formed. Their parents thought it was little more than a club, but the boys had actually solved some important mysteries.

"Here's a case for your amateur detective firm," Mrs. Crenshaw went on. "Get my father safely to New York, and I'll make it worth your while."

Jupiter grinned. "It's not the sort of case we usually take on," he pointed out. "We're detectives, not bodyguards."

"You could regard it as valuable experience," said Mrs. Crenshaw. "You don't want to keep doing the same old thing all the time, do you? You'll get stale."

Jupe looked toward Bob and saw a hopeful gleam in his eye.

"I'm for it," Bob said.

"It would be a challenge, I suppose," said Jupe.

"You don't know what a challenge it could be," said Pete. "Grandpa on the warpath is not to be believed."

"And he will be on the warpath," predicted Pete's mother. "He's convinced that creative people like himself are often treated rudely, and he resents it deeply. So if you could keep him from running amok and doing damage to whatever people he comes across, I would be forever grateful."

The wall telephone rang.

"Oh, dear!" exclaimed Mrs. Crenshaw. "I don't think I really want to answer that."

"I'll get it, Mom," said Pete.

The others heard him say hello and then, "Are you sure?" He listened a moment and said, "Just a second, huh? I'll tell her."

He turned to his mother. "It's Mr. Castro,

Grandpa's friend from across the street. He was supposed to play chess with Grandpa today, but when he went over to Grandpa's house, no one was there. He said the back door was standing open and the water was running in the kitchen sink. He thinks we should call the police."

"The police?" said Mrs. Crenshaw. "That's silly. Pop's just gone on an errand. He'll be back soon."

"Mom, his car is parked in the driveway, but he isn't there. And would he go out and leave the door open? And the water running?"

"Oh, dear. Well, all right. I'll go over."

It was then that Jupiter stepped in. "We'll go instead," he offered. "You want to hire The Three Investigators, and now we have something to investigate. You wait here. We'll call you from Mr. Peck's house."

The three boys rushed eagerly out the door, wondering what kind of trouble Pete's grandpa was in this time.

2

Encounter with an Enemy

Mr. Castro was pacing in front of Mr. Peck's house when the Three Investigators rode up on their bikes. He was a skinny, nervous man, with a fringe of gray hair and a brown, wrinkled face, and on this bright spring day he was terribly agitated.

"This isn't like your grandpa," he said to Pete. "We were going to play chess, and he would never miss this game if he had his druthers. He lost the last time we played, and he wants to get even. Your grandpa doesn't like to lose."

"That's for sure," Pete agreed.

The boys went in through the front door, which was unlocked. Mr. Castro trailed after them, twitching with apprehension. "I just know something awful has happened," he said. "Your grandpa would never go off and leave the water running and the back door standing open."

The Investigators were drawn to the kitchen, where they stared at the sink as if it could tell them something.

"He was going to boil some water," said Jupiter. "See, the kettle's there on the counter with the lid off. And while he was at the sink, he looked out through that window above the sink, and he saw . . . something."

Jupe looked through the window now, and he wondered what Mr. Peck had seen. He himself could see a strip of Mr. Peck's side lawn, and a neatly trimmed low hedge that separated Mr. Peck's lot from the next property. Beyond the hedge was a yard that appeared weedy and neglected. The house next door was a forlorn structure with paint peeling from the window frames and several shingles curling up from the roof.

"Who lives there?" Jupe asked Mr. Castro.

It was Pete who answered. "A guy named Snabel, but Grandpa couldn't be there. He and Snabel hate each other. There's a battle every time they meet."

"That may be," said Jupiter, "but somebody went through that hedge, or over it, very recently. See where several twigs are broken there? The wood under the bark still looks white, which means that the breaks are fresh."

The boys went out then, and across the yard to the hedge.

"It's low enough for Mr. Peck to have stepped over," said Jupiter. "He could have accidentally snapped those twigs as he did."

Mr. Castro groaned. "The last time Ben Peck went over to Ed Snabel's yard, Snabel threatened to shoot him. Mrs. Milford across the way called the cops, and Ben and Snabel both filed charges. Ben said Snabel swiped his lawn mower and Snabel said Ben tried to break into his garage. Eventually they both dropped the charges, but things got pretty ugly for a while."

"Then it would be wise to persuade Mr. Peck to leave Mr. Snabel's property," said Jupe. "Supposing, of course, that that's where he is—and I think it is."

Jupe stepped over the hedge then himself, breaking some more twigs, and Pete and Bob followed him. Mr. Castro hesitated, but at last he came too, and the four of them started a circuit of the shabby house.

They did not have to go far. Beyond the house was a garage, and beyond the garage was a small glass and wood structure—a greenhouse. It was not neglected like the big house. The wooden trim was white and freshly painted, and the glass panes in the walls and roof looked clean, although they were fogged with mist.

Suddenly, from the far side of the greenhouse, there came a gleeful, malicious little song:

"Run as fast as you are able.
I've got you now, you rotten Snabel!"

"Oh, good grief!" cried Pete. "Grandpa?"
"What?"

Mr. Bennington Peck peered around the corner of the greenhouse. He was a slender, wiry man who looked remarkably spry and erect for his age. Mr. Peck was flushed with virtue and his blue eyes sparkled. "Pete, my boy! And Jupiter! And Bob! Come see what I've found. Oh, Castro, I beg your pardon. We had an appointment, didn't we? I'm sorry. I'm afraid I've kept you waiting."

"For quite a while," said Mr. Castro. "I wanted to send for the police, but your family thought that was premature. Peck, what in tarnation are you doing?"

"I am trying to get this greenhouse door open," said Mr. Peck. He demonstrated, prodding the lock with a penknife.

"Ed Snabel will have the law on you!" warned Castro.

"Grandpa, you scared us!" Pete said.

Mr. Peck looked contrite. "Oh, I'm sorry, Pete. I didn't mean to do that. But get close to this glass and look in. See what's there!"

"Grandpa, Mr. Snabel's going to get you for breaking and entering."

"Nonsense! I haven't broken anything. I am simply trying to get the door open so that I can retrieve what is rightfully mine. You see that can? It's malathion! The same malathion I bought at Harper's last week. I was going to spray my Chinese elm, but suddenly the malathion was gone! And that's the trowel I thought I'd lost. It had a notch on the handle. So Snabel not only swipes lawn mowers, he makes off with trowels and insecticide too. And he spies on me. What he wants with a lawn mower when he never mows a lawn, I'll never know! Does it just to be spiteful. I'll bet when he drags his orchids around to clubs and tells other orchid nuts what a great fellow he is, he doesn't mention that he's too cheap to buy his own supplies!"

Mr. Peck gave a vicious jab at the greenhouse lock with his penknife.

"Grandpa, you can't be sure those things are yours," said Pete.

"I know my own trowel when I see it!" insisted Mr. Peck. "I've been missing it and the malathion. And I saw the broken twigs in my hedge. I'm not so old that I can't put two and two together anymore, you know."

Just then they heard a car pull up in Snabel's driveway. A pudgy, dark-haired man appeared from around the corner of the garage. He had deep-set eyes under heavy brows, and he was scowling fiercely.

"Ed Snabel, you've been in my toolshed again!" Mr. Peck accused. "You open up this greenhouse and give me back my trowel and my malathion."

"You're a meddling old fool," said Snabel. "You ought to be locked up. Now get off my property or I'll call the police, and this time I won't drop the charges!"

Mr. Peck snapped his penknife shut. Then he waggled the closed knife at Snabel. "I'll let you get away with it this time," he said grandly, "but if I catch you snooping around my yard again, I'll take care of it myself, and the devil take the police!"

"Grandpa, please!" pleaded Pete.

"Don't pester me, boy!" said Mr. Peck. "I won't stand for being pestered—not even by my own flesh and blood!"

Mr. Peck stamped away from the greenhouse. The Investigators trailed him across the yard, and

Mr. Castro brought up the rear. Castro looked weak with relief.

"I sometimes hate coming here," groaned Castro. "It's like entering a war zone."

"That creep!" Mr. Peck said as he stepped back over the hedge and strode toward his house. "We ought to have a neighborhood association, like they do in some of those cooperative apartments. Then we could vote on who might buy property and who wouldn't be allowed."

"It would be unconstitutional, I expect," said Mr. Castro. "Besides, they might vote against you!"

"Don't be ridiculous!" cried Mr. Peck. "And I wish you'd stop wasting time, Castro. Do you want to play chess, or don't you?"

Mr. Castro made a noise that sounded like a pot boiling over, but he followed Mr. Peck into the house. Mr. Peck filled the kettle at last and put it on to boil. Then Mr. Peck and Mr. Castro went to the living room, where the chessboard was already set up.

There was a telephone on the kitchen counter. Pete picked it up and dialed his home number. He wanted to tell his mother that all was well, at least for the time being.

"Do you think we could keep him out of trouble if we went along on that trip?" said Pete to Jupe. He kept his voice low.

Jupe looked doubtful. But then he brightened and grinned. "It wouldn't be easy," he said, "but it certainly wouldn't be boring."

Jupiter understated the case. He had no way of knowing that The Three Investigators were about to experience one of the wildest adventures of their lives.

3

The Adventure Begins

The week after the uproar about the garden supplies, Mrs. Crenshaw invited her father to dinner. She served all of Mr. Peck's favorite dishes, including a super-rich chocolate cake with a whipped cream frosting. When Mr. Peck—and the three Crenshaws—had eaten, Mrs. Crenshaw poured the coffee and then suggested casually that Pete and his friends would find a coast-to-coast car trip very educational. She was almost sure she could arrange their early release from school if Mr. Peck agreed to take them with him when he left for New York.

Mr. Peck looked stunned.

"Come on, Pop," said Mrs. Crenshaw. "Remember the trip we took the year I was ten? You and

19

Mom and I went to Carlsbad Caverns, remember? It was so wonderful! I've never forgotten it. And it would mean just as much to Pete if he could go with you. And if Jupe and Bob came along, Pete wouldn't be a bother. You wouldn't have to worry about the boys. They're very responsible."

Mr. Peck stirred his coffee and looked searchingly at his daughter. She recognized that look. It meant he could see right through her.

Mrs. Crenshaw felt her face go red, and she began to fold her napkin into nervous little pleats.

"You think I need a guardian," said Mr. Peck. "Yes, the boys are responsible. They would make excellent guardians."

"Pop, it isn't that at all. It's just that since you are going to drive all that way, and . . . and kids don't often get a chance to . . . well, it seems a shame . . ."

"To waste the gas?" said Mr. Peck.

He turned to Mr. Crenshaw, who had been carefully saying nothing. Mr. Crenshaw did not like to argue with Mr. Peck. It wasn't that he always lost when he disagreed with his father-in-law. It was just that neither of them seemed to win. Arguments did not end in peace treaties, but only in truces. There was always the promise of a new battle to be fought another day.

But Mr. Crenshaw could not avoid this discussion. "You think I need a guardian?" Mr. Peck asked his son-in-law now.

Mr. Crenshaw took a deep breath and decided to level with the old man. "Most of the time, no," he said. "But if I have to drop everything and fly to Indiana or Idaho, well, I just—"

"Who said you're going to have to fly to Indiana or Idaho?" cried Mr. Peck. "Why should you? To get me out of jail, I suppose. The way you two talk I've been in jail every Saturday night for the past forty years. May I remind you that I have been arrested—actually arrested—only once, and that was because I wouldn't let those know-nothings from the Parks Department destroy my tree. Since then, you act as if I'm mad, or a criminal, or worse. Well, I'll tell you what I think—"

He stopped and glared at Pete, who had been sitting silently, hardly daring to breathe.

"I think it's a great idea for the boys to come along!" announced Mr. Peck. "It *is* a long drive, and I'll want someone to talk to. Boys are better than old codgers like Castro or Harry Jacobson. Castro takes a special suitcase for his medications when he travels. And Jacobson retired to get away from the insurance business, but now all he can talk about is insurance. Phooey! So if Pete and his pals can square it with their folks and with the school, that would be just fine. In fact, since there are only a couple of weeks left before school lets out, I'll put off my trip till then. If we leave early in June we can cross the plains before the worst of the heat, and maybe we can come back through Canada. Would you like that, Pete?"

Pete jumped up. "Wow!" he cried. "Would I!"

He flew to the telephone to call Bob and Jupiter.

Bob had a fairly easy time persuading his parents to let him go. They had great faith in the maturity of the Three Investigators—especially Jupiter—and thought it would be a wonderful chance for Bob to see the country. In the days that followed, Bob arranged for a temporary leave from his part-time job at the Rocky Beach Library.

Jupe was an orphan who lived with his aunt Mathilda and uncle Titus Jones, owners of The Jones Salvage Yard. Aunt Mathilda and Uncle Titus hesitated only slightly before giving Jupiter permission to take the trip. Jupiter pointed out to them that to cross the continent not once but twice would be the adventure of a lifetime. "Great experiences shape the character," said Jupiter pompously, "and it will be a great experience."

"Your character is shapely enough already," said Aunt Mathilda. However, she went up to the attic, got out a sleeping bag, and spread it on the lawn to air it out.

Jupiter followed her like a shadow.

"You mean I can go?" he said.

"I wonder what the weather is like in June in Minnesota," said Aunt Mathilda.

"Beautiful!" cried Uncle Titus.

Jupiter's face lit up. "I promise I'll finish the inventory of the salvage yard before I go," he said.

"I just wish I could join you on the trip," Uncle Titus said regretfully. He had been a calliope player with the circus in his younger days. Sometimes he still longed for the excitement of circus life and the journeys across the country.

"Somebody has to stay at home to tend to the business," said Aunt Mathilda, with a smile.

Jupiter worked through the cool spring afternoons and the lengthening evenings to finish the inventory.

The time went by and the last day of school finally rolled around. Then the boys were in a sudden fever of packing and saying good-bye. On a foggy June morning Mr. Crenshaw deposited the boys and their suitcases on Mr. Peck's lawn. The boys had no sleeping bags—Pete's grandfather had firmly vetoed the proposal that they all camp out. "I am too old to play boy scout," Mr. Peck declared. "This may be the last grand adventure of my sunset years, and I intend to go in style. We are staying in hotels and motels, and we are going to be comfortable."

At last all the boys and the luggage were stowed inside Grandpa's aged but sturdy Buick. They were off. Pete looked back to wave to his father before they turned the corner, and so did Jupe. Both boys saw a stocky figure come silently around the side of Grandpa's house and stand half-hidden in the bushes, watching the departure.

It was Edgar Snabel.

"He isn't losing any time prowling around Grandpa's place, is he?" murmured Pete.

"What'd you say, Pete?" cried his grandfather from the front.

"Nothing, Grandpa," said Pete quickly. "I was just wondering if we could stop for something to eat at that great place in Santa Barbara. You know, the one with tables in the courtyard?"

"You've got it," said Mr. Peck. "I'm hungry already. Funny how breakfast doesn't stay with you when you eat too early. Or did I eat this morning? I don't remember."

Mr. Peck headed for the Pacific Coast Highway in high spirits, and Jupiter grinned. The first small challenge had been met. The trip might be serene after all.

But in his heart of hearts, Jupe didn't believe that. He knew the stubborn, excitable Mr. Peck too well. With him at the wheel, anything could happen—and probably would.

4

The Man in the Fog

The second breakfast in Santa Barbara was a feast. The Three Investigators and Mr. Peck ate in the courtyard of a building that dated back to the days when California was a Spanish colony. The sun had come out and the fog had wafted away. The air was clear and fresh.

"Glorious!" cried Mr. Peck. "And it will get even better. You'll see!"

They went on, speeding north, sometimes driving level with the surf and the beach, and sometimes speeding along the tops of cliffs so that they looked down at the sea. A few miles beyond Gaviota they plunged into a tunnel. On the other side of it was a different sort of country. They saw cattle instead of surf. The pastures were still green after the winter rains, and mustard plants were in bloom, powdering the green with gold. Here and there little calves frisked on the slopes, and colts raced about the meadows.

It was early afternoon when they again caught sight of the sea.

"Pismo Beach!" said Mr. Peck. "When I was younger, Pete, before your mother was born, your grandmother and I used to come to Pismo on weekends and dig for clams. Haven't done that for years. Clams don't seem too exciting to me now, but it would still be fun to drive down onto the beach."

"You mean take the car out on the sand?" asked Bob. "You can do that?"

"You can at Pismo," said Mr. Peck. "Let's see if I can find the place."

He drove off the highway, wandered up and down side roads and into dead ends, and at last came to a ramp that led from the end of the street onto the hard-packed sand beside the ocean.

"We won't get stuck?" asked Pete. He tended to distrust some of his grandfather's ideas. "You promise?"

"I promise," said Mr. Peck. "Look over there."

He pointed toward a Volkswagen that was speeding along the beach just above the water line. Now and then a wave broke close to the shore and the little car splashed through surf, sending sheets of water flying up.

"Swell!" said Pete. "But aren't Volkswagens supposed to be waterproof? Suppose the Buick stalls."

"You worry too much," said his grandfather.

Pete sighed. He knew he was a worrier, but with Mr. Peck in the family how could he avoid it?

The Buick negotiated the ramp, then rolled smoothly across the beach. There was fog offshore again. "They get a lot of fog here for some reason," said Mr. Peck. He stopped the car, set the parking brake, then turned toward the boys.

"I need to stretch my legs," he said. "Anyone for a walk?"

"You bet," said Pete.

All four doors popped open at once. The boys got out, Mr. Peck locked the car, and they set off down the beach. In minutes they passed the town of Pismo Beach. It was a cluster of close-set buildings that crowded toward a retaining wall. Beyond the town were cliffs that were crowned by hotels and motels.

The fog was nearer now, closing around them slowly, beginning to blot out the view of the beach ahead. The air took on the haunting quiet that comes with fog. The boys knew that the highway was just beyond the clifftop hotels, but they could hear no sound of traffic.

The beach stretched ahead, almost deserted. A solitary figure came toward them, walking briskly. Then suddenly the fog grew more dense and the lone walker disappeared. The world was a gray, chill blank all around them.

Jupe felt a foreboding, a sense that something dangerous lurked in the mist—something that could seize them and carry them away somewhere, that could muffle any shouts for help.

He shook himself. It was nothing, he knew. There was no threat here, only the harmless fog that had blotted out the sun and made the beach seem dank and unfriendly.

"Haven't we gone far enough, Mr. Peck?" said Bob.

He was ahead of Jupe, hurrying slightly to keep up with Pete, who was taller and more athletic. Bob looked to his right where Mr. Peck had been walking. Mr. Peck was nowhere to be seen.

Pete stopped. "Grandpa?" he called. "Hey, where are you?"

Still there was no answer.

"Mr. Peck?" cried Jupiter.

They waited for a second, then Jupe announced that there was nothing to worry about. Jupe spoke in his most confident way, but he felt a surge of anxiety even as he attempted to reassure Pete.

Where was Mr. Peck? He couldn't simply disappear into the mist—or could he?

"Let's stay close together, huh?" said Pete. He was barely more than a silhouette beside Bob. He touched the smaller boy on the shoulder, as if to keep Bob from vanishing into the gloom.

"Mr. Peck?" Bob called.

"Grandpa, where are you?" Pete was pleading now.

"Be quiet!" said the familiar, grumpy voice.

A sudden breath of wind parted the fog for a moment. The Investigators saw Mr. Peck. He was crouched beside a boulder at the foot of a cliff, and he looked tense and watchful.

"Grandpa, what's the matter?" Pete whispered.

The old man made shushing motions at him.

"Aha! I thought so!" growled Mr. Peck at last. He sounded absolutely outraged.

The solitary stroller whom the boys had seen on the beach was nearer now—quite near, in fact. He stepped along carefully, groping and stumbling a bit in the fog.

"Scoundrel!" cried Mr. Peck. He leaped from behind the rock and threw himself at the shadowy stranger.

The man staggered back, uttering a half-strangled cry.

"How dare you?" shouted Mr. Peck. He seized the man by the shirt front. "How dare you follow me here?"

"Watch it, you maniac!" yelled the stranger.

"Oh, my gosh!" gasped Pete.

"Peck, you crazy old coot!" yelled the man. "You let go of me or I'll wring your scrawny throat!"

The voice was dreadfully familiar. It was Ed Snabel, Mr. Peck's detested neighbor.

Mr. Peck did not release his enemy. Instead, he gave the man a shake. "You two-faced snooper!" he raged. "I know what you're up to. You found out my latest invention, didn't you, by creeping around when honest people are in bed! It isn't enough that you swipe my tools. You want to swipe my ideas, too. Well, just because you've got a brain like a dried pea—"

The man broke free and stumbled back away from Mr. Peck. "You lunatic!" cried Snabel. Then he raised his voice and shouted, "Police! Help! Murder!"

"Mr. Snabel, please!" Pete thrust himself between his grandfather and Snabel and clung to Snabel's arm. "Please, my grandfather didn't mean it. He's just—"

"Don't you dare!" shouted Ben Peck. "Don't you dare apologize for me! I meant every word of it. I know what this spineless parasite is doing, and he won't get away with it. I'll turn him in, that's what I'll do!"

Again Mr. Peck tried to seize Snabel. This time Snabel did not shout. He backed off stiffly, keeping his eyes fixed on Mr. Peck's face.

"Spy!" Mr. Peck taunted him. "Sneak! Swindler! And why aren't you at work where you should be on a Thursday, eh? Because you think there's more to gain someplace else, don't you?"

Snabel turned and stumbled away down the beach.

"The truth hurts, doesn't it?" Mr. Peck cried after him.

But Ed Snabel was gone, swallowed up by the fog, safe from the terrible old man who now raged and fumed.

"Incredible!" snorted Ben Peck. "Outrageous! If he tries that again, I'll really put the fear of God into him!"

Pete found that he was shaking. It was a nightmare, and his grandfather was mad—totally, stark crazy. He was dangerous. He would wreck the trip before they even got to San Francisco. He would wind up in jail in one of the towns along the coast. Or perhaps Jupiter and Bob would decide that they had taken on an impossible task, and would pick up their gear and catch the next Greyhound bus back to Rocky Beach.

"Grandpa," said Pete at last, "why do you think Mr. Snabel would follow you here? I mean, that's so weird. He's got a right to take a trip too, doesn't he? Maybe he's got friends here in Pismo Beach, and he came to see them."

"Tommyrot!" snapped Mr. Peck. "Snabel doesn't have friends anywhere. He wouldn't know a friend if someone shipped one to him wrapped in colored paper. You mark my words, we haven't seen the last of him. But he won't get what he's after. I'll die first!"

"What is he after, Mr. Peck?" asked Jupiter. He managed to sound as if he could be convinced, and this calmed Mr. Peck.

"He wants to steal my idea," said Peck.

"The invention?" said Pete. "The one you're going to show to those people in New York?"

"Of course. And don't say it like that, as if I were some crackpot. It's an important break-through. It could revolutionize the whole . . . whole—"

He stopped suddenly. "No," he said. "For your sakes it would be best if I didn't explain further. Snabel may not be the only one who wants it. And we'd better be on our way if we're going to reach Monterey before dark."

He sauntered off down the beach, suddenly as calm and unconcerned as if nothing had happened. The Three Investigators followed slowly, each wondering about the old man. They were setting out on a long journey. They would be gone for a month at least, and possibly even longer. Was Pete's grandfather just an uninhibited eccentric, or were they crossing the country with a man who was truly insane?

5

Something's Fishy

"On this trip," said Mr. Peck, "I do not plan to share a room with anyone. Boys are always wanting bizarre things like glasses of water or even crackers and cheese at three in the morning, and I am too old to be rattled awake by such nonsense."

Having made this announcement, Mr. Peck booked two rooms at a motel a few blocks from Fisherman's Wharf in Monterey. He then treated the boys to a fine fish dinner at one of the restaurants on Cannery Row. He talked with great good humor about Monterey and Spanish California. The encounter that had taken place with Snabel seemed long ago and far away, and certainly not important. Mr. Peck had obviously put it out of his mind.

The Investigators went to bed early that night. They realized very soon that Mr. Peck had made the right decision about the rooms, but for the wrong reason. If he had chosen to share a room with them, *they* would have been rattled awake all night long. Pete's grandfather snored with such vigor that the wall between their two rooms vibrated.

"He's got a sinus problem," Bob decided.

"Mom says he doesn't," Pete countered. "Mom claims he doesn't like to be ignored, even when he's unconscious."

But with the wall between them and the old man, the boys soon tuned out the snores. They dropped off to sleep and did not wake until the morning sun came in through the crack between the drapes.

Mr. Peck was already up. They could hear his shower running. He sang as he splashed around, and they had to hurry to be ready when he rattled the doorknob of their room.

Breakfast was sausages and waffles and a pitcher of orange juice in a place near the wharf. Jupiter tended to be quiet in the morning. He was eating stolidly and steadily, and gazing out the window toward the bay, when he suddenly recognized a passerby. The man was just crossing the street in front of the restaurant. Jupe couldn't help giving a slight start. Then he dropped his eyes to his plate and began to mop up a puddle of syrup with a bit of waffle.

Pete was sitting opposite Jupiter and next to his grandfather. He noticed Jupe's start and the quick change of expression, and he opened his mouth to ask a question. Jupe frowned and shook his head slightly, and Pete closed his mouth again.

"Have you had enough, Jupiter?" Mr. Peck asked.

"Yes, thank you, Mr. Peck. It was very good."

"It was great!" said Bob.

Mr. Peck pushed his chair back and went to the cashier's desk to pay the check.

"What's the matter, Jupe?" Pete leaned forward. "You looked so . . . so funny there for a second."

"Snabel is here," said Jupe.

Pete looked toward the window. "Here? You sure?"

"He went past us and down toward Cannery Row," said Jupe.

Mr. Peck came back to put a tip on the table. "Want to take a quick turn around the wharf?" he said. "Then we should be on our way. I'd like to get past San Francisco tonight—maybe drive as far as Santa Rosa. Then we can spend tomorrow in the redwoods."

The three boys followed Mr. Peck out and across the street. Bob had his camera, and he wanted to take some pictures of the bay. He led the way to a spot near the end of the wharf where he would have a clear view of the boats bobbing at their moorings and the yachts skimming across the bay bound for the open ocean.

It was still early, but Fisherman's Wharf was already busy. Tourists wandered in and out of the shops that sold seashells and imported knick-knacks. Bob snapped his photographs and Pete watched the gulls circling overhead. Mr. Peck gazed idly into the window of a shell shop.

Then Mr. Peck glanced down the pier toward the street, and he stiffened.

"The wretch!" he cried.

Jupe knew without looking. It was Snabel. It had to be. He had reappeared, and Mr. Peck's cheery mood had disappeared. In its place was fury.

"Hey, Grandpa," said Pete. "Take it easy, huh? It's a free country. The guy has a right to be here if he wants to."

Mr. Peck sniffed furiously. "Very well. But I refuse to be here at the same time!"

Mr. Peck then ducked into the shell shop and crouched behind the huge abalone shell that was displayed in the window. The boys could see the top of his white head, but nothing else.

Snabel came along the wharf, calmly unaware that he was under observation. He had a camera bag over his shoulder, and he carried the camera in his hands. It was a Canon II, the twin of Bob's camera. Like Bob, Snabel appeared to be looking for picturesque things to photograph. He was the typical tourist that morning, with his shirt open at the neck and his jeans stiff and new. He was wearing new sneakers as well, and somewhere along the way he had acquired a broad-brimmed straw hat. It now shaded his face.

Pete hesitated. Should he warn Snabel that his grandfather might pounce at any moment? If he did that, Mr. Peck would regard it as a betrayal. Pete did not want to watch another confrontation between Mr. Peck and Snabel, but he also did not want to draw his grandfather's wrath down on his own head.

Pete turned at last and looked out across the bay. Jupe did the same. And Bob walked a yard or two down the pier to a bench. He sat down facing the bay and pretended not to see Snabel.

Snabel came along with his camera. He stopped so close to Pete that their shoulders almost touched. But Snabel did not notice Pete. He kept looking back the way he had come and glancing at his watch, as if he was waiting for someone.

After a minute or two someone approached.

"Well, Snabel?" said a man's voice.

There was amusement and a hint of disdain in the newcomer's remark. Jupe turned his head and glanced at the man. He saw a person somewhere in his forties, with a head of smooth dark hair. He had a smooth face too, and silk slacks and a soft shirt that looked fashionable and expensive. The man wore sunglasses that concealed much of his face, but Jupe saw a high, thin nose and thin lips that curved in a mocking half-smile. Small ears were set close to the man's head. The total effect was that of a sleek person accustomed to having the best. Next to this splendid individual, the chubbier Snabel looked stiff and awkward in his new jeans and very white sneakers.

"I brought it," said Snabel.

The newcomer glanced at Jupiter.

Jupe turned to gaze innocently across the bay.

"Over here," said the man to Snabel. He walked a few paces down the pier, and Snabel rustled along with him.

Again Jupe peeked at the men. The two were quite close to Bob now. Snabel was plainly trying to appear casual. He put his foot up on the end of the bench where Bob sat, and he dangled his camera by the strap.

And suddenly his eyes focused on Bob, who was trying to make himself invisible.

"What the devil!" said Snabel. He bent and stared squarely into Bob's face. Jupe was sure Snabel went pale.

He straightened up and looked around, and he saw Pete and Jupe. He also saw the fringe of white hair above the abalone shell. Then Mr. Peck rose up in all his awful fury, his blue eyes snapping. Snabel went dead white.

"Great!" said Pete. He started toward Snabel, thinking he would get between Snabel and the shell shop, but he was too late. Mr. Peck dashed out of the shop, his face crimson. His fists were clenched as if he were going to beat Snabel to within an inch of his life.

Snabel quickly let his camera down onto the bench and flung his hands up. At first the boys thought he was going to strike out. He didn't. He merely took a step or two backward and kept his hands up in a defensive way.

The elegant person in the silk slacks simply melted away and was gone.

"Hah!" cried Ben Peck. He again took a handful of Snabel's shirt. "Didn't think you'd see me quite this soon, did you? Well, I know what you're up to, Snabel, and I'm not going to let you do it. Wise up! Knock it off while you still can."

Snabel wet his lips. He tried to say something, but his voice came out in a gurgle. Then he coughed.

Oddly, he did not try to push Mr. Peck away. He did not try to step back or strike out or run. He only gaped at Mr. Peck. His face was a dreadful color.

Mr. Peck let go of Snabel's shirt, but he rapped smartly on Snabel's chest, rather as if Snabel were a door. "Take my advice and walk off now, or you'll be sorry for the rest of your life."

Well-satisfied with the effect he had produced, Mr. Peck turned cheerily to the boys. "Let's be on our way," he said. "The neighborhood's been going downhill fast in the last few minutes."

Pete discovered that he had stopped breathing. He started again.

Bob grabbed his camera from the bench.

The Three Investigators followed Mr. Peck down the wharf and across to the parking lot where they had left the Buick. Mr. Peck was chuckling as he unlocked the doors and got in, and he laughed out loud as they rolled out onto the street and turned toward the highway.

Someone shouted behind them. It was Snabel. He was chasing after them, his straw hat in one hand and his camera in the other. "Wait!" he yelled. "Peck! Just a second!"

Mr. Peck stepped hard on the accelerator and the car spurted ahead.

"Grandpa, what was that all about?" asked Pete.

"What do you think it was about?" said his grandfather. "That miserable leech who has been trying to get into my house is now tailing us because he thinks I've got my notes and my prototype model right here. He wants to get hold of my invention and claim it for his own. Fat chance! I'd see him in jail before I'd let him get my things."

"You're going to see him in the hospital with a heart attack if you do that again," warned Pete. "He was scared to death. Grandpa, you keep on acting this way and you'll be the one in jail. And Mom will have my hide!"

6

Pete Spots Trouble

"When Grandpa's okay, he's really okay!" said Pete. "I mean, who else would want to drive all the way across the country with a bunch of kids? And he seems to like having us along.

"But when he gets crazy . . . it's scary!"

Jupe nodded. He had known Mr. Peck for years, but he had never spent so much time with him before. Jupe was shocked and puzzled by some of his actions. The First Investigator did not often let grownups get the better of him, but Mr. Peck was in a class by himself. Jupe was sure now that they were in for more trouble before the trip was over— real trouble!

It was 1:30 in the afternoon. Jupiter and Pete were leaning on the fender of the Buick and watching Mr. Peck. He and Bob had scrambled part of the way up the grassy slope above, and Bob was busy snapping pictures. Mr. Peck was gazing happily at San Francisco Bay and the Golden Gate Bridge. He was in high good humor. Pete hoped that the mood would last.

Actually, Mr. Peck's anger had been brief that day. He had muttered and grumbled only until they were on Highway 101. Then thoughts of Snabel had vanished like mist before the sun, and Mr. Peck had begun to whistle. They had sped north to San Francisco and had stopped there for lunch and some souvenirs. Over lunch Mr. Peck had told the boys tales of the great San Francisco earthquake of 1906.

"The city burned almost completely, didn't it?" Jupiter said.

Mr. Peck nodded. "The water mains and the gas pipes ruptured during the quake, and when the gas caught fire, there was no water to fight the flames."

He looked at his watch then and announced that it was time they were moving on.

It was after two when they crossed the Golden Gate Bridge. They left the highway at Sausalito and drove up into the hills and stopped so that Bob could take some more pictures. They were still there at half past two when Bob discovered that he had used up the roll of film in his camera.

"That's weird," said Bob. "I could have sworn I had a lot more exposures left on that roll." He jogged down the hill and got his camera bag from the back of the car and changed the film. Then he took a few more shots.

They went back to the main highway, and then north through the pleasant countryside. The sun was edging to the west as Mr. Peck drove.

They stopped at Santa Rosa at dinnertime, and Mr. Peck took two adjoining rooms at a motel there. The rooms had a connecting door. Mr. Peck joked about keeping tabs on the boys.

"I guess on this trip we all watch out for each other," said Pete. He was gloomy again, but only for a minute. His grandfather suggested a swim in the motel pool, and he brightened up. Dinner in the motel dining room cheered him even more, and after dinner he felt only a pleasant drowsiness as he and Bob and Jupe watched television in their room.

Pete decided to buy a soda at the machine down by the pool. On his way to the door he passed the window. When Pete glanced out of it, he immediately forgot about his soda.

The Investigators' room was on the second floor

and overlooked the parking area. Pete saw rows of cars on the macadam below. The Buick was there, almost directly beneath the balcony in front of their room, and beyond the Buick was a shining new Lincoln.

Edgar Snabel was just getting out of the Lincoln.

Pete caught his breath. For a second he was motionless, shocked and paralyzed. Then he spun around and said, "Jupe, Bob, get a load of this."

In a flash the other two Investigators were at Pete's side. Through the window they could see Snabel slowly circling Mr. Peck's car. He bent and looked in through the windows. Then he went to the back of the car and tried the lid of the trunk. Then he looked back toward the motel office and up at the windows above him.

The three boys shrank out of sight.

Snabel frowned, then got into his Lincoln and drove off.

For a moment no one said anything.

"Perhaps your grandfather's suspicions are correct," Jupe said at last. "Perhaps Snabel *is* trying to steal ideas from him."

Pete shook his head. "I-I just don't know. I took it for granted that that was just another one of Grandpa's wacko ideas. But maybe he isn't such a flake. Or maybe he's crazy and Snabel is too. But . . . let's not tell Grandpa we saw Snabel. He'd be sure to go charging down to the local police station to get Snabel arrested. The cops might wind up tossing *Grandpa* in a cell—you never know!"

"You never do," agreed Jupiter. "Not where Mr. Peck is concerned."

"You know, it could be a coincidence," Bob added. "Snabel could be on vacation too, and he happened to wander in here. Then he saw Mr. Peck's car and decided it would be better to spend the night someplace else."

"Hey, that reminds me," Pete said. "Where did Snabel get a brand-new Lincoln? He drives a beat-up old Chevy."

"Maybe he rented it," said Jupiter. "He may have thought his old car couldn't weather the trip."

With that the Three Investigators went back to watching television. Mr. Peck came in to watch with the boys for a while. At ten thirty they declared that the day had officially ended and they put out the lights.

Mr. Peck fell asleep promptly, and soon his snores thundered from the next room. Bob sighed and Jupe chuckled. As for Pete, he got up to close the door between the two rooms, and then went back to his bed and dropped off eventually.

He had a dream that was strange, and yet wretchedly familiar. In the dream he was following his grandfather through a hotel lobby. It was a large lobby thronged with stylish, well-dressed people who stared and pointed and laughed at them. Pete was suddenly aware that his grandfather was striding along wearing only a red undershirt and white underpants with red hearts embroidered on them. As for Pete, he was wearing nothing at all!

Pete woke with a shudder. It was pitch black and very quiet, and Pete thought it must be very late. He slid out of bed and started for the bathroom to get some water. On the way he passed the window.

Again there was someone walking slowly, stealthily behind the row of parked cars. Pete froze.

The shadowy figure crouched beside the Buick. "Jupe!"

Pete flew to Jupe's bed and shook him. "Jupe," he whispered. "Quick! Wake up! It's Snabel. He's down in the parking lot messing with our car!"

7

Circle of Terror

Barefoot, the Three Investigators dashed down the outside stairs.

Jupe stumbled, making a thumping sound on the stairs. He caught at the railing to keep from falling.

The figure that was crouched beside the Buick straightened, shot one quick look at the stairway, then dashed down the line of cars toward the street.

The boys chased after him, limping in their bare feet. When they reached the street, the prowler was gone.

"Rats! We lost him!" cried Bob.

"Thanks a lot, Jupe," said Pete.

"Are you sure it was Snabel?" Jupiter asked, ignoring the sarcasm.

"Positive," Pete declared. "I caught a glimpse of his face when he ran past one of the porch lights."

The boys padded back to the Buick. They circled it, checking the doors. The doors were still locked. So was the trunk. Jupe got down on his hands and knees and peered at the underside of the car, but he could see nothing.

"I've got to get the flashlight," he decided.

A door opened above them and Mr. Peck came out onto the balcony.

"What's going on?" he demanded. "It's almost four o'clock in the morning!"

It was meant to be a whisper, but Mr. Peck's whispers could carry for half a mile. Lights went on in the motel wing across the way and several guests looked out.

"Somebody was prowling around down here," said Pete.

"Snabel, I'll bet!" said Mr. Peck.

Pete did not confirm this, but he did not deny it either. Mr. Peck ordered the boys upstairs, and when they were back in their room he grumbled and muttered about Snabel. "He suspects what I've got," he declared. "Well, he won't get it!"

"What *do* you have, Grandpa?" asked Pete.

"Never you mind," said his grandfather. "The less you know, the better off you are. Now you boys get back to bed and finish your sleep. No

sense letting that polecat keep you up. So long as
he hasn't done any harm. He hasn't, has he?"

"We don't think so, Mr. Peck," said Jupe.

Mr. Peck nodded. "Just his style—slinking and
sneaking, but no real action!"

Mr. Peck went back to his bed, and in a sur-
prisingly short time he was snoring again.

"I hope Grandpa's right," worried Pete. "But
what if Snabel is up to more than a little sneaking
and spying? What if he plans to damage the car?
Put it out of commission or something? I'm going
to sleep down there tonight, just in case he comes
back."

Pete took the blanket from his bed and crept
into his grandfather's room. Without disturbing
Mr. Peck's thundering snores, Pete lifted the car
keys from the bureau. Then he and Jupe went
down the stairs. They got the flashlight from the
glove compartment, but nothing happened when
they flicked its switch.

"Rats," said Pete. "Dead batteries. I don't get it.
What was Snabel trying to do, anyway?"

"Whatever it was," said Jupiter, "he didn't suc-
ceed. Okay, now, if he shows up again, you yell."

Pete promised that he would—at the top of his
lungs—and Jupe went back up the stairs. Pete
crawled into the back seat of the Buick and curled
up, sure that he would not sleep another wink.

He did sleep—but restlessly—and he had more strange dreams. When he woke again, the sun had just come up, the birds were chirping in the trees, and a chubby woman in a purple jogging outfit was knocking on the car window.

"You all right?" called the woman.

Pete sat up—and slipped off the seat onto the floor.

Alarmed, the woman yanked at the door handle, but Pete had locked the doors before going to sleep.

"I'm okay!" cried Pete. "Thanks, but I'm okay!"

He pulled the blanket around him to cover his pajamas, then opened the door and stumbled out.

"What are your parents thinking of?" scolded the woman. "It isn't safe to sleep outside like that!"

"Yes, ma'am," said Pete.

He fled up the stairs and rattled the doorknob so that Bob or Jupe would let him in.

"Imagine!" said the woman to herself in the parking area. "Some people will do anything to keep from paying for an extra room!"

Bob opened the door and Pete went inside. "Let's not tell Grandpa a thing about this," he said. "He'd have a fit if he could hear that lady."

"He sure would," Bob said, laughing.

They drove north on the Redwood Highway

that day. Mr. Peck was in a sunny mood. The giant trees on either side of the road reminded him of earlier trips he had taken—trips he had made when his wife was alive.

"You don't remember your grandmother too well, do you?" he said to Pete.

"Just a little bit," said Pete. "She used to make the greatest apple cake, I remember that."

"She did indeed," said Mr. Peck. "It was good for what ailed you."

Jupe watched the old man, and he reflected that Mr. Peck was really two different people. One was the loving, enthusiastic grandfather who could treat his grandson and his friends to a fantastic trip. The other was a cantankerous old codger who harbored exaggerated suspicions about a neighbor. Though at first Mr. Peck had seemed really crazy, now Jupe had to admit that there was a grain of truth in his accusations. Edgar Snabel really had been prowling around the Buick. Was it because he hoped to get his hands on one of Mr. Peck's inventions? Or was there some other reason for his actions?

Jupe wondered for perhaps the hundredth time what Mr. Peck's new invention might be. He knew better than to ask, however. Mr. Peck was determined not to tell. He did not object to talking about

Snabel, though, and Jupe thought the Three Investigators might learn something if only Mr. Peck would talk enough.

"I wonder about the orchids," said Jupe suddenly.

"Orchids?" Bob stared at Jupe. "What orchids?"

"Doesn't Mr. Snabel raise orchids?" said Jupe.

"Yep," said Mr. Peck.

"Mr. Snabel doesn't seem to be someone with the patience for gardening," said Jupiter. "He doesn't even cut his lawn."

"That's because there's no money in cutting a lawn," said Mr. Peck. "Not unless you're a professional gardener. Snabel's not interested in plants—he just likes money. He has plenty of time for his orchids because they're worth a lot of money. Florists buy them from him. He belongs to an orchid club, and once a month he gets together with a whole bunch of other orchid nuts to compare plants. I'll bet he swipes supplies from them too."

"Who's taking care of Snabel's orchids now?" Jupiter asked.

"Maybe one of the club members," said Mr. Peck. "I must say that I'm not losing any sleep over it.

"Did you know that when he was new on the block, I had my water shut off for a while? The Department of Water and Power found a leak between the main out in the street and my house.

While they were fixing the leak, I had no water. So I went over to Snabel's with a teakettle to borrow some water from the faucet on the outside of his house. Do you know what happened?"

"He called the police?" suggested Bob.

"He threatened to," said Mr. Peck. "He also accused me of attaching my hose to his faucet when he wasn't home and using his water to water my lawn! As if I'd do such a penny-pinching trick as that!"

The back of Mr. Peck's neck was now very red, and for the first time that day Mr. Peck was paying no attention to the redwoods.

"Snabel is obviously paranoid," he declared. "That's why he thought I'd steal his water. You know what paranoid is? It's when somebody is so sick in the head that he imagines everybody else is out to get him. Snabel is paranoid!"

Jupiter was somewhat daunted by the force of Mr. Peck's anger. He decided that he had heard enough about Snabel for the present, and he made no more remarks to draw Mr. Peck out on the subject of his unpleasant neighbor. For a time they drove on in silence.

But the day was too pleasant and the redwoods too awe-inspiring. Mr. Peck forgot his anger and again began to reminisce. His happy humor lasted all the way to Crescent City, California.

The sun was low when they pulled into that little seaside town, so they checked into a motel and washed up. Then they set out to explore the marina nearby.

The little wharf was much simpler than Fisherman's Wharf in Monterey had been. There was parking on the quay, however, and several restaurants and one or two stores. Across from the restaurants were the slips where sailboats tied up. The place was busy enough, with the boatmen tinkering and cleaning and touching up. Couples strolled slowly along the pavement, enjoying the sunset and watching the gulls.

"We seem to have lost Snabel," said Mr. Peck suddenly.

Pete felt a pang of anxiety. His grandfather had not mentioned the unpleasant orchid-fancier for hours, and he had hoped that Mr. Peck had forgotten Snabel. But Peck hadn't.

"I was watching the road behind us in the rear-view mirror," he told the boys. "Nobody seemed to be sticking to our tail. You boys must have scared that polecat off last night when you spotted him near our car."

"I sure hope so," said Pete earnestly.

He turned toward the highway then, for there was a roar of motors and some yelling.

Seven motorcycles sped onto the quay. The bikers were all burly young men in black leather jackets.

"Hmm!" said Mr. Peck. "Tough-looking crew."

They were. In addition to the black leather, most of them had beards—either full, tangled growths that threatened to crawl up into the bikers' eyes, or strange, bristly beards trimmed into odd shapes. The bikers were decked out in belts and leather wristbands that were studded with nailheads, and gloves that flashed with studs.

"Hey, Grandpa!" yelled one of the men. He swooped at Mr. Peck on his bike, then skidded away.

The boys expected a burst of rage from Mr. Peck. It did not come. Instead the old man looked after the bikers and grinned. "I'm sure some nice people ride motorcycles," he said, "but none of them are with us today."

"Grandpa, let's go, huh?" coaxed Pete.

The bikers had rumbled out to the end of the quay. They clustered there around the biker who had tried to scare Mr. Peck, and they looked back at Mr. Peck and the boys in a calculating way.

"C'mon!" Pete tugged at his grandfather's sleeve. "Let's get out of here."

"Eeeee-yaaa!" yelled one biker.

A bike roared and the same man was speeding straight back at Mr. Peck and the boys!

"Stay close!" shouted Mr. Peck, and he stepped forward to meet the biker's charge.

Jupe felt his stomach go tight with fear. Behind the lead bike, the other riders were coming, sneering—and laughing mockingly. One of them swung something in the air. It was a belt—a cruel strap studded with bits of metal.

All around the boys, the sightseers and strollers scrambled away. "Call the cops!" yelled someone.

The bikers roared past Mr. Peck, then swerved and turned and came back at him. Their laughter was louder now.

Then the riders surrounded Mr. Peck and the boys in a circle. Moving constantly, they made the circle smaller and smaller, getting steadily closer to the prey trapped inside. It was a game—a horrible game!

"Get 'im!" yelled one of the men, and he wheeled out of the circle and sped straight at Mr. Peck. At the last possible instant he stopped short.

The boys saw dark little eyes gleaming above the man's beard and square little white teeth in a smudged face. They heard his laughter even above the roar of the other bikes.

Then Mr. Peck moved. It was such a slight movement the boys almost missed it. Mr. Peck had thrown something.

A shot rang out, and there was a puff of smoke—

thick, black smoke that billowed up around the attacking cycle.

The little eyes went wide. The grinning mouth opened in a yell. The biker jumped, and then he turned his bike so sharply that it fell over.

Mr. Peck threw again. Again there was a sharp explosion, and again the thick smoke.

The bikers moved back, bewildered, looking this way and that, wondering where the gunman could be.

Sirens wailed down the highway. Two police cars turned onto the quay with roof lights flashing.

"Shall we eat now, boys?" said Mr. Peck.

He started briskly for one of the restaurants on the wharf. The boys trotted after him.

The doorway of the restaurant was crowded with people who had watched the action on the quay. They stepped aside to make room for Mr. Peck.

"You okay?" One man put a hand on Mr. Peck's shoulder.

"You don't want to fool around with those guys," said another onlooker. "They can be mean!"

"Young man, I was not fooling around," Mr. Peck announced. "If the officers had not arrived just then, those thugs would have found out how serious I can be!"

8

Dangerous Days

Mr. Peck stared out of the restaurant window. He saw the policemen on the quay confronting the bikers. The bikers were reluctantly showing their driver's licenses.

"If I weren't anxious to get on with our trip I'd sign a complaint against those lowlifes," said Mr. Peck. "I'd charge assault, and I'd see them in jail where they couldn't menace anyone else for a while." He opened a menu.

Outside on the wharf, the cyclists had started their bikes. They wheeled about in a group and rode slowly down the pier. The officers got back into their cars and followed.

"Do you think they're going to jail?" said Bob.

"I doubt it," Mr. Peck said. "I expect the police will follow them out of town, and good riddance."

"Grandpa, what made that noise?" asked Pete.

"Noise?" said Mr. Peck. "What noise?" He was concentrating on the menu; he seemed to have forgotten the bikers.

"You threw something at the guy who was going to run you down, and it went off like a gun. What was it? A firecracker?"

"Certainly not!" Mr. Peck said, bristling. "Fireworks are illegal in many areas. That was one of my minor inventions. I hope it will be a commercial success once I get it on the market. It's a simple device that makes a loud noise, produces a puff of smoke, and is entirely harmless and legal. It could be marketed to the public as an anticrime measure. It could frighten muggers and holdup men out of their wits."

Pete grinned. "If it scares a biker, it'll scare anyone. But what happens when the word gets around and all the muggers and holdup men know the gadget is harmless?"

"Then I'll sell it to postal workers," said Mr. Peck cheerily. "You have no idea the amount of trouble they have with ill-mannered dogs."

And with that, Mr. Peck turned back to the menu and decided on the red snapper for his dinner.

It was after 1:00 p.m. the next day, and they had passed Portland, Oregon, when Pete sighted the sign beside the road.

"Hey, Grandpa, there's a viewpoint for Mount St. Helens. Can we stop?"

"Of course," said Mr. Peck. "How many active volcanoes can one see in a lifetime? Never let an opportunity slip by, that's what I always say."

He turned off the interstate highway and the car climbed into the hills, higher and higher on a twisting road. The day turned grayer than it had been, and all at once there were wisps of cloud trailing across the road.

They came to the viewpoint at last, and they knew that they would have to imagine Mount St. Helens. They were above the lowering clouds now, and when they looked toward the east, where the mountain had to be, they saw dense gray billows and nothing else.

"Rats!" said Pete.

Mr. Peck grinned. "Never mind. We have the whole great country ahead of us, and it's filled with wonderful sights."

He turned the car and they started back down to the interstate. Before they reached the main road again, rain was spattering the windshield.

On Highway 5 some of the cars had headlights on. Mr. Peck immediately decided that they would stop that night in Longview, Washington, and not attempt to go farther. He was so involved with his plans that he did not notice the Lincoln parked on the shoulder of their side of the road. It showed no lights, but the windshield wipers flicked back and forth and a plume of exhaust rose in the dank air.

Jupe stiffened at the sight of the car. As they passed it and merged into the northbound traffic, he stared back.

Someone was hunched over the wheel. Was it Snabel? The car looked like the one Snabel had driven in Santa Rosa, but Jupe could not be sure. He knew that there had to be hundreds of gray Lincolns on the road. Almost automatically he made a mental note of the license number: 920-XTJ.

"Snabel!" Mr. Peck hissed suddenly. Without warning he hit his brakes. The car that was behind them on the highway blasted its horn.

"Grandpa, watch it!" yelled Pete.

Mr. Peck accelerated again, just as the car behind them swerved and braked. The collision did not happen. The boys were shaken, however, and Mr. Peck was contrite.

"Sorry about that," he said. "That parked car we passed back there . . . I barely glimpsed him, but I could swear it was Snabel."

The boys looked back. The Lincoln was still there

beside the road, its grayness melting into the grayness of the rainy day.

"He isn't following us," said Jupe. "He's just parking there as if he's reading a road map or . . . or maybe he's disabled."

"Snabel could still follow us. If he's got any brains at all he could figure we'll be on this road at least as far as Seattle. He could be trying to lull our suspicions."

After that they drove on in silence. They turned off early that day and cruised the streets of Longview until they found a small motel on a side street. Mr. Peck decided it would do; it was far enough from the highway. Snabel would never locate them here.

"Not that I like it," said Mr. Peck. "I never ran from a fight in my life, but I could make a career out of fighting Snabel. I can settle with him later. The important thing is to get to New York safe and sound—and if possible to have a good time on the way."

Like Mr. Peck, the Three Investigators weren't used to running from problems. But in this case running seemed the only thing to do. If Snabel *was* pursuing them, they could do nothing until he made a move. If Mr. Peck had only imagined that Snabel was after him, the boys could deal with it best by simply sticking close to the old man.

That night Jupiter awakened sometime after midnight. He heard Mr. Peck snoring heartily in the next room. But it was not the snores that had disturbed Jupiter; he had grown used to the snores. It was the brightness of headlights as someone turned slowly into the motel driveway and then stopped.

A car door opened, although the driver did not kill the motor. Footsteps hurried on the ground outside and then stopped, and then hurried again.

Jupe got out of bed.

A car door shut as Jupe hurried to the window. When he peeked out he saw a big car turn onto the street.

Was it the Lincoln? He could not be sure.

He went back to bed, and he told himself sternly that he was getting as eccentric as Mr. Peck. Soon he would be seeing Snabel crouched behind every bush, or trailing after them on every highway. It was ridiculous. And even if Snabel was following them along their route, what did he hope to gain? He hadn't ever damaged their car or ransacked their rooms.

And what about the invention that Mr. Peck planned to present in New York? Where was it? Unless it was small enough to fit into a suitcase, Jupe could think of no place in the car where it might be hidden.

Jupe dropped off at last, and when he woke, Bob and Pete were already up and dressed. He had to hurry.

They drove east that day across Washington, climbing to cross the Cascade Mountain range, and then coming down to a great plain that was rather barren.

"It's a desert!" said Pete. He sounded terribly disappointed. "I thought the whole state of Washington was piney woods."

"Looks like you thought wrong," said his grandfather.

But beyond Spokane they were in mountains again, and sometimes streams rushed along beside the road and the forest closed in around them.

That night they stopped at Coeur d'Alene, Idaho. Mr. Peck again insisted on a small, out-of-the-way motel like the one they had used in Longview, Washington. Once again they all thought of Snabel.

But Mr. Peck was quite cheerful. "Maybe we've lost him," said Mr. Peck. "I've been watching in the rearview mirror all day, and I didn't spot anything suspicious. Not that it would do to take any chances. We'll stay here, and if he's still behind us he'll figure either that we stopped in Spokane or that we'll go on to Missoula."

Pete hoped fervently that Mr. Peck's preoccupation with Snabel might be coming to an end. And it seemed to be. Mr. Peck said no more about his neighbor during dinner and the lively evening of miniature golf that followed. He ended up with the best score and drove the boys back to the motel well pleased with himself.

That night, after they were all asleep, a high, whining whistle shrilled through the building.

"Now what?" Pete said, sitting up.

The whistle went on and on, earsplitting, piercing. Pete sniffed, and then he yelled.

"Jupe! Bob! Get up quick!"

He pounded on the wall to wake Mr. Peck. "Grandpa! That's the smoke alarm! The motel's on fire!"

9

Smoke Screen

Eeeeee! The shriek of many smoke alarms pierced the night.

The Investigators could hear people running and shouting. Car doors slammed. The air was thick with smoke.

Jupiter sprang to the phone and called the fire department.

Pete dashed outdoors in his pajamas and began to pound on the door of Mr. Peck's room. "Grandpa! Grandpa! Get up! The motel's on fire!"

Coughing from the fumes, Grandpa staggered to the door.

Eeeeeee!

By then Bob had his jeans on and was outside, too, knocking on doors, waking up the guests.

A woman in a pink chenille robe opened the door, rubbing her stinging eyes. "Wha?" she mumbled.

"The motel's on fire," Bob told her.

With that she jerked awake.

"Norman, get up! I told you we should never have stayed in this dump!" she yelled into her room.

By this time all three Investigators and Mr. Peck were banging on doors around the U-shaped building. Smoke billowed around them. It seemed to be coming from the end of one of the wings.

There was a crash and the tinkle of breaking glass. In the courtyard parking lot a car with Indiana license plates had backed into a car with Oregon plates. The Oregon driver stuck his head out his window. "Watch where you're going, you dummy!" he yelled.

The guests kept pouring out of their rooms, coughing and clutching their robes to ward off the chill. Some ran for their cars and a quick escape; others gathered in the courtyard to watch what would happen.

"Did anybody call the fire department?" one woman asked.

"Yes," said Jupe, "they're on their way."

"Look at that, Jupe," Pete said.

At one end of the U-shaped building was a door

marked EMPLOYEES ONLY. Smoke poured from the cracks around the door.

"That's it, all right," Jupe said quickly. "Everybody stand back, away from the fire."

Pete and Bob moved the other guests away from the door.

At that point the roar and wail of the fire engines could be heard, coming up the street.

"What's going on here?" said a bald little man in an old bathrobe. "I'm the manager." He carried his keys in one hand and a fire extinguisher in the other.

"The fire seems to be behind that door," Jupe began.

The manager was already unlocking it.

"Wait!" Jupe cried. "Don't open that door!"

It was too late. The key turned in the lock. The door swung out. A sheet of flame shot from the doorway, and the motel manager staggered back and dropped the fire extinguisher. His arms went up to shield his face. A wave of intense heat passed over the boys.

Pete ran to help the man, and Bob grabbed the extinguisher. He turned it upside down and directed a stream of liquid foam at the blaze in the tiny room inside.

Two fire engines arrived at the front of the motel. Firemen ran and shouted, and in seconds

Bob was thrust aside. A fireman aimed a hose at the flames and a powerful jet of water roared into the little enclosure, and then it was all over. The fire was out. The smoke alarms ceased to shriek. There was nothing to see in the little storage room but a few charred mops and brooms, a plastic bucket that had melted out of shape, and a sodden black heap of wet rags on the floor.

A fireman went into the little room and scowled at the wet mass at his feet, then kicked it. He picked up one of the rags and sniffed. "Oil of some kind," he announced. "Smells like turpentine. You been painting?"

The question was directed at the motel manager, who was now missing his eyebrows. "No!" said the man. He clasped his hands as if he were praying. "No indeed! Haven't had any paint around the place for weeks—months!"

The fireman sniffed again. "Furniture polish?"

"No!" said the manager. "It couldn't be. I mean, I don't allow the help to leave oily rags around."

"You could have fooled me," said the fireman. He dropped the blackened rag to the floor.

Mr. Peck snorted accusingly from a few feet away. "You wouldn't have these problems if you used Furglow," he said.

"Furglow?" echoed Bob.

"It's one of Grandpa's inventions," Pete explained. "Specially treated disposable pads. You polish furniture with them, then you throw them out."

"I sold the idea to one of the soap companies, and they put it in a safe somewhere and forgot it!" said Mr. Peck bitterly. He stamped off to his room, and an instant later he shouted as if he had been bitten.

"Rotten, thieving sneak!" he yelled. "Pete! Jupiter! Bob! You come here!"

The boys went.

"Check your room, quick!" yelled Mr. Peck.

He was standing in his doorway glaring at his bed. It had been torn apart. The mattress was folded up so that one end was doubled over the other, and the blankets were heaped on the floor. Mr. Peck's shirts and underwear and socks were strewn about, and his toilet kit had been upended on the bureau.

Jupe gaped. For an instant he didn't move. Then he stepped around Mr. Peck and went into the bathroom. There was a window high over the tub in the rear wall of the building. It was open, and some scuff marks on the tub showed where someone had stepped on the porcelain with shoes on.

Jupe got up on the edge of the tub and examined the window latch. The paint was chipped there.

"Somebody shoved the latch open and got in through the window," Jupe told Mr. Peck. "He may have gone out the same way, or perhaps he went out the door. It would have been easy for him to escape in that crowd, with all the excitement and the smoke."

Bob came running from the room next door. "Hey, you guys, you know what?"

"Yeah," said Pete. "Somebody's been in our room, tearing the place up."

Bob nodded. "Right. But as far as I can tell, nothing's missing."

"Snabel!" cried Mr. Peck. "He tracked us here!"

"How, Grandpa?" said Pete. "Even if that was his car parked by the lookout turnoff yesterday, we haven't seen it since. How could he know we were here?"

"He could be sticking to our tail," insisted Mr. Peck. "Suppose that was a rented Lincoln he had. He could have turned it in and now he'd be driving something else."

Jupiter remembered seeing a big car the night before outside the motel in Longview, but he kept his thoughts to himself. There was no need to excite the old man any more.

Pete surveyed the wreckage of the room. "Grandpa, aren't you going to check to see if he got your invention?"

"He didn't get it," said Mr. Peck. "He won't get it, either."

Mr. Peck stamped back out to the courtyard and the boys followed.

Some of the guests still waited there, watching the motel manager fidget and fuss. The fire engines waited on the street, engines rumbling, and a patrol car was parked in the driveway. The light on top of the car whirled, so that flashes of orange light flicked across the front of the building.

Mr. Peck marched toward the policeman who stood in the doorway of the storage closet conferring with one of the firemen.

"You don't need to wonder about it," Mr. Peck told the two men. "That fire was set."

The fireman and the officer looked at him with cautious curiosity. "You know something about it?" said the fireman.

"You bet I do!"

Pete sighed. "Here we go again," he told Jupe.

"Ed Snabel set that fire," said Mr. Peck. "He did it so he could get into my room and search it. I just discovered my room and the boys' room completely torn apart. The man's got no conscience. He endangered a whole bunch of people just to get what he wants. This place could have burned to the ground, and he wouldn't have batted an eyelash!"

The motel manager beamed at Mr. Peck as if the old man had just descended from heaven riding on a white cloud. "I told you!" he cried. "I told you we never have oily rags here. The cleaning people have strict orders. So it wasn't carelessness, it was arson!"

The officer stepped into the supply closet and squinted at the window in the far wall. It was like the one in Mr. Peck's bathroom, and it hung halfway open, the latch broken.

"How long's this been this way?" asked the officer.

"Never was like that before," declared the manager. "I keep things locked up, and I keep things in good repair. I wouldn't allow a window latch to stay broken more than an hour or two."

The officer turned to Mr. Peck. "I'd like to see your room," he said.

Peck was happy to show it. Then Jupiter, Pete, and Bob showed their room.

The officer made notes. His partner came from the car and began knocking on doors, asking questions of the guests who had gone back to their rooms. Soon the partner reported that Mr. Peck's room and the boys' were the only rooms that had been entered.

"It could have been a hotel thief," said the first officer, "but they don't usually operate like this, and—"

"It was Ed Snabel, I tell you!" declared Mr. Peck. "He followed us here from Rocky Beach—"

"Rocky Beach?" said the officer.

"It's in California. Listen, he was waiting for us at Pismo Beach and again at Monterey. For all I know he set those motorcycle thugs on us. I want him arrested. He's dangerous!"

"Yes, sir," said the officer. "And why is he following you? Why did he tear up your room? What's he looking for?"

"My invention," said Mr. Peck.

"Oh?" said the officer. "What invention?"

Mr. Peck froze. A look of cunning came to his face. "I-I don't think I can tell you that," he said. "I can't tell anyone just yet."

"I see," said the officer. "Well now, if you could describe this man, and his car, we could—"

"He was driving a Lincoln, but by now he's probably got something else," said Mr. Peck. "Why are we standing here yammering? He's getting away!"

The officer nodded. He smiled soothingly, then took Mr. Peck's name and his home address, and the names and addresses of the boys. He also wrote down the license number of the Lincoln when Jupe gave it to him. Then he got into the patrol car, and he and his partner drove away.

"Blasted moron!" said Mr. Peck. "He's not going to do anything, I can tell."

"He thinks we're crazy," said Pete. "Grandpa, let's face it. If Snabel *is* following us, we're on our own!"

10

Panic in the Park

It was two days later. Mr. Peck and the boys had driven across Idaho to Livingston, Montana, and then south to Yellowstone National Park in Wyoming. Traffic on the roads was sparse so early in the season. In Yellowstone they saw steam wafting from cracks in the ground, and they watched geysers spurt scalding water more than a hundred feet into the air. They stared amazed at pools of bubbling mud, and lost count of the beautiful lakes and waterfalls. Awed by the wonders of nature in this once volcanic area, the travelers forgot their worries for a while.

But then Pete turned to look back at the park road, and Bob sighed. Pete was watching for the enemy.

"We haven't seen anything suspicious since that turnoff to Mount St. Helens," said Bob.

Jupiter decided the time had come to break his silence. He told them about the large car he had seen pulling out of the motel driveway in Longview.

"Of course, I have no proof whatsoever that the driver was Mr. Snabel," Jupe admitted.

"Maybe Snabel's back in Rocky Beach by now, watering his orchids," Bob said. "Maybe that fire in the motel was just a coincidence. We happened to check into that place on the night some thief decided to fake a fire and rob the rooms and—"

"Poppycock!" snapped Mr. Peck. "That was no ordinary thief who searched my room, or yours either. Nothing was taken. My wallet was on the bedside table, and the sneak who broke in didn't touch it. He didn't take your camera, either."

"He couldn't have taken my camera," said Bob. "It was in the car. I forgot to take it out that night."

"But my money?" persisted Ben Peck. "I've heard about hotel thieves—they can spot money so fast it would make your head spin. And they don't go around setting fires to create a disturbance. That's not the way they operate."

The exhilaration the boys had experienced watching the geysers had dissipated by now. Once again they felt a dull foreboding.

"We'd better get going," said Mr. Peck. He too was edgy again. "This place is too empty. Makes me nervous."

Under ordinary circumstances Pete might have said, "Oh, Grandpa, come off it!" Today he was not sure his grandfather was off base.

Late in the day they checked into a motel in a small town near the Montana–Wyoming state line. Once they had brought their luggage into their rooms, Mr. Peck drove the Buick away. He parked the car on a side street and then spent the rest of the evening trudging back and forth from the motel to the car to make sure the Buick was still undisturbed.

"You're defeating the purpose of parking the car out of sight," Pete said after his grandfather's fifth trip to the car. "If Snabel really is following us, he might spot you going back and forth like that. Then all he has to do is follow you back here and—whammo!—our motel rooms will be redecorated again, free of charge."

That sent Mr. Peck back to his room, where he was soon sleeping noisily. The Three Investigators lay awake and speculated about the fire in Coeur d'Alene.

"Couldn't be Snabel who did that," Pete insisted. "Not unless he really has ESP. We'd have noticed a car on our tail—any car!"

"Maybe he's got a helicopter and is tracking us from the air," suggested Bob.

"Where would he get a helicopter?" Pete retorted. "Besides, helicopters are noisy. We'd have spotted him."

Jupe suddenly sat up in bed. "We'll call him!" he announced. "Why didn't I think of it sooner? We can call his house in Rocky Beach, and if he answers we'll know it was all a coincidence, and we have nothing to worry about."

"Do you know his number?" said Bob.

"Of course not, but unless his telephone is unlisted, information will have the number."

Jupe reached for the telephone on the table next to his bed. A minute later he was listening to the ringing of Edgar Snabel's telephone.

"He'll be mad if we wake him," said Bob.

"It's an hour earlier in Rocky Beach," Jupe pointed out. "We're in the Rocky Mountain time zone now."

After the phone rang three times there was a click as if a receiver had been lifted at the other end. Jupe heard an empty silence and then a second click.

"I'm sorry," said a recorded voice. "This is Ed Snabel. I'm not able to come to the telephone right now. If you'll leave your name and a number where you can be reached, I'll get back to you as soon as

I can. Wait for the tone before you leave your message." That was followed by an ear-shattering bleat.

"Darn!" said Jupe. He put down the receiver. "He has an answering machine."

"So we know as much as we did before," said Pete.

"We can try to call again in the morning," Jupe said. "Perhaps he'll answer then."

But when Jupe tried to call Snabel at 8:00 a.m., the answering machine clicked into action again and the Investigators gave up.

They felt weary and discouraged when they first started out. The day was clear and beautiful, how-ever, with a wide blue sky that was dappled with little puffs of cloud. They drove across Wyoming through miles and miles of pasture land where cattle grazed. As they approached Rapid City, South Dakota, Mr. Peck announced that he was not going to let Snabel ruin their vacation.

"We are going to have a good time in spite of that tubby twerp," said Ben Peck. "We aren't going to miss any of the things we want to see."

The boys rallied at this, and they were noisy with laughter over lunch in Rapid City. Then they managed to drive all the way south to Mount Rush-more without looking back once. Jupe did notice, however, that Mr. Peck glanced more often into the rearview mirror than was absolutely necessary for safety.

The road to the observation platform at Mount Rushmore curved and wound up and up for several miles, and then leveled out at a parking area where they left the car. Mr. Peck and the boys continued on foot up a broad walk where the flags of fifty states floated in the wind. It was an easy climb of perhaps a quarter of a mile from the parking area to the deck. There they could stand and look across pine-covered slopes at the gigantic faces of four great presidents which had been carved into the stone of the South Dakotan mountainside.

"What a project!" said Pete.

Jupiter had a guidebook with him. "The colossal heads of Washington, Jefferson, Lincoln, and Theodore Roosevelt were created under the direction of the late Gutzon Borglum," he read. "Each face is sixty feet high."

Pete chuckled suddenly. "Maybe when he was little his mother told him to grow up and do something really big so she could be proud of him."

"How clever!" said a voice behind the boys.

Pete looked around, and so did Mr. Peck.

"Your grandchildren?" said a chubby lady in too-tight jeans. She beamed at Mr. Peck.

"One of them is," said Mr. Peck.

"Children are so precious!" the woman gurgled. "They have such fresh, original ideas!"

Mr. Peck looked at the boys as if he were trying to discover signs of their freshness and originality. Pete glowered and Bob went red.

Jupiter, who hated to be called a child, sent a hard stare at the woman. She looked as if she was in her late fifties. She wore a shirt with neon-pink roses embroidered on the yoke. She also wore pink earrings and pink lipstick that exactly matched the roses. She smiled stickily and took a step or two toward Mr. Peck.

"My one regret," she said with gentle disappointment, "is that I never had children. Everyone says I should have. 'Bessie,' they say, 'you'd have been a marvelous mother.' But I do so enjoy other people's youngsters."

Mr. Peck found himself looking into her eyes from a distance that was much too short to suit him. He tried to take a step back away from the lady and discovered that she had taken hold of his sleeve. She wore pink nail polish; it was the same color as the lipstick.

Pete looked at his watch and cleared his throat. Then he said, "Grandpa, we've got to get going. Grandma's waiting for us back at the motel."

It was an effective lie—as good as anything

Jupiter had ever thought up. The woman's rosy cheeriness vanished. She took her hand off Mr. Peck's arm and moved away from him.

"Oh, dear!" she said. "I mustn't keep you. It's been so nice chatting."

"Hasn't it!" said Mr. Peck. He smiled gallantly and started away toward the parking lot. The boys closed around him like bodyguards and protected his flanks.

"Grandpa, you son of a gun!" crowed Pete when they were safely in the car. "That lady wanted to move right in on you!"

Mr. Peck grinned and stuck his chin out. "There's life in the old boy yet!" he boasted.

They drove out and down the slopes, and then turned off on the road that led to nearby Custer State Park.

"One of the largest bison herds in the world lives in Custer State Park," said Jupe. "I've seen bison in zoos. I've never seen one in the wilderness."

"It will be a slice of life," said Mr. Peck. "Jupe, did you swallow that guidebook before we set out? Or do you stay up nights memorizing chosen pages?"

"It's that steel-trap mind of Jupe's," said Bob. "He never forgets a fact."

"I wish I could say the same thing," declared

Mr. Peck. "I have days when I'd forget my name if it wasn't on my driver's license."

"That's because you're so busy hanging around with us, sopping up all our fresh, original ideas," said Pete, "like the lady said."

"True," said Mr. Peck, "and if you get any fresher, I'm going to drop you off on the side of the road and you can walk to Custer."

They sped down a hill and went slowly through a gate into Custer State Park.

Mr. Peck suddenly said, "Good night, what are *they*?" and stopped the car.

A herd of wild donkeys was gathered by the road. Their delicate little hoofs clop-clopped on the pavement as the animals came over to the car windows.

"I think they want us to feed them," said Pete.

"Terrific!" exclaimed Mr. Peck. "They're probably hooked on junk food. I hope the bison won't be looking for a handout."

The bison were not. The great shaggy animals were grazing some distance inside the park, and they ignored the car when Mr. Peck stopped on the road.

"Once there were so many bison that the plains were black with them," said Jupiter. "They used to wander over the railroad tracks and hold the trains up for hours."

"And now these are almost the last bison left," said Mr. Peck. "Shows what humans can do when they set out to shoot things."

Bob was snapping away with his camera. "I'd like to get closer if I could," he said. "From this distance they're going to look like so many boulders in the tall grass."

"Forget it!" warned Pete. "Those things are dangerous."

"They certainly are," said Mr. Peck. "Every year some darn fool tries to pose next to one and he gets gored. Let 'em be. They're wild animals, and wild animals are always dangerous."

When they had left the bison behind, they found a place where they could pull off and park beside the road.

"I've been sitting long enough," said Mr. Peck. "I'm ready for a short hike." He pointed to a trail that led up away from the road into the pine-covered hillside. "Anybody game to see what's at the end of that trail?"

"So long as the end isn't too far away," said Bob.

Mr. Peck took the keys from the ignition. "You coming?" he asked Jupiter.

"I don't think so," said Jupe. "I think I'll stay here and just think for a while."

Mr. Peck shrugged. "Suit yourself."

He and Pete and Bob hiked off, and in a few

minutes they had disappeared into the dense woods. Jupe got out of the car and listened.

There was another car coming up the road. Jupe waited, half expecting a gray Lincoln to appear. It was not the Lincoln that came into sight, however, but a camper with an elderly man at the wheel. The man waved to Jupe as he went by.

Jupe smiled, realizing he was letting his imagination get the better of him. No one was following them. Had Snabel been on their tail, he would have had to keep them in sight at least part of the time. They had been alert and watchful, but had seen nothing suspicious for hundreds of miles.

A bird called out from a tree above Jupe, then flew off with a whir of wings. Jupe decided that he was bored waiting there beside the road. When the others left he had had the thought that he needed to guard the Buick, but surely that was foolish. He would hurry and catch up with Bob and Pete and Mr. Peck.

He started up the trail.

The woods closed around him, and when he looked back at the first bend in the trail he could not see the road. He heard a car engine, however. When that sound stopped he heard a car door open, then close.

Someone had pulled off the road and parked next to the Buick.

Jupe felt his breath come faster. The hair on the back of his neck prickled. He took a step sideways and looked around. The person who had parked near Mr. Peck's car was starting up the trail, and Jupe was swept by a sudden panic. He had to hide!

The hillside was quite dark, shadowed by the trees that covered it. Underbrush was sparse. But a few yards to the right of the trail there was a clump of some low bushy shrub that resembled manzanita. Jupe made for it and threw himself down behind it. He peeked toward the trail, looking past the roots of the plant.

Jupe could not see the newcomer's face but he could make out a pair of feet that trudged into view. There was some hoarse, labored breathing. The newcomer stopped, facing straight up the path. He wore brown loafers and jeans. Jupe theorized that the man might be someone who wasn't used to the outdoors. The loafers were quite new, the jeans looked stiff, and the man was resting there for a long time.

Why was he waiting so long before going on? Had he noticed something? Had Jupe left some sign when he stepped off the trail?

All at once Jupe felt terribly exposed. If the man turned to his right, he would surely see Jupe.

Suddenly something wild broke from cover off

to the man's left, and the man turned that way, looking to see what had made the noise.

In that moment, Jupe raised himself swiftly on his hands and knees and looked out over the top of the shrubbery.

He almost gasped.

The stubby figure on the trail had a gun in his hand!

"Yoo-hoo!" someone called.

The man on the trail looked down toward the road. Now Jupe could see the man's face under his broad-brimmed straw hat. And now he was sure. It was Snabel.

Jupe dropped to the ground. He was sweating. Did he dare make a run for it? He decided he did not. Snabel would surely see him if he left the sparse shelter of the shrub.

"Remember me?" said the voice on the trail. It was a woman, and she was quite near now. Jupe grinned. He knew that voice. It was Bessie, the woman who had spoken to Mr. Peck at Mount Rushmore.

"I thought I'd never see you again," she said. "After lunch you just seemed to disappear into thin air!"

Jupe decided that Snabel must have put the gun in his pocket, out of sight. He heard Snabel mumble something about having to get gas, and he heard the woman express delight at finding Mr. Snabel again. She offered to accompany Mr. Snabel on his hike, if hiking was the thing he had in mind. Mr. Snabel declined brusquely, saying that he had had all the fresh air he needed for one day. Then Snabel and the lady started back to their cars, with the woman emitting an endless, meaningless stream of chatter.

Jupe raised his head and looked after them.

The woman was holding Snabel's arm as he tramped stolidly along, so unresponsive that he might have been a robot in that determined grip. Jupe guessed that Snabel was furious at being overtaken and made prisoner by the lady.

The unlikely pair disappeared. A minute or two later Jupe heard one car start, then another, and the two drove away.

Jupe found a rock to sit on, for he could feel his knees shaking under him. He couldn't wait to tell the others.

11

A Daredevil Move

Jupe's friends found him sitting beside the trail when they returned half an hour later.

"You missed a swell hike," said Pete.

Bob frowned. "Something's happened," he said. "You look . . . you look weird."

"I never dreamed he'd come after us with a gun," said Jupe. He shook his head. "It was a shock. And Mr. Peck, we all owe you an apology."

"You do?" said Ben Peck. "Why?"

"Snabel was here," said Jupiter, "and he had a gun. Until now, I've had doubts about your suspicions. But you were right. He is trailing us, and if he can he'll do us real harm."

Jupe then told them about seeing Snabel on the trail.

Ben Peck chuckled at the end of Jupe's story. "Well, that woman does like to take up with strangers, doesn't she. Snabel's about as strange as they come; he should keep her occupied for a while."

Pete glared at his grandfather. Mr. Peck was absolutely rosy with cheer.

"Grandpa, it isn't funny," said Pete. "We could all have been shot. Now that we know, maybe we ought to call the cops, or the sheriff, or whoever you call around here."

Mr. Peck shook his head. "You remember that officer at the motel fire, when I told him about Snabel? He thought I was crazy. You said it then, and it's true: Whatever happens, we're on our own. Now let's not stand here fussing about it. Let's get on with our trip!"

He took a deep breath, as if savoring the wilderness for the first time. "I think I'm relieved," he said. "Now we're sure. You know, I was beginning to wonder myself if maybe I wasn't getting kind of senile."

Jupiter and Pete exchanged a surprised look. Mr. Peck tramped on down to the car and the boys followed him. They drove back to Rapid City in the twilight and checked into a motel. After a hamburger dinner at the nearest fast-food place, Mr. Peck went to bed and snored triumphantly.

Jupe went to bed and stared at the ceiling. "How does he do it?" he wondered.

"You mean Snabel, or Grandpa?" asked Pete.

"Snabel," said Jupe. "He seems able to home in on us no matter where we go."

There was no answer for this, and the others didn't attempt one. In time they were all asleep.

When they set out the next morning everyone was tense. They watched the road ahead and then looked back frequently. Whenever they stopped at various viewpoints on their tour of the South Dakota Badlands they stayed close to the Buick. The weird spires of rock in the Badlands made Pete especially uneasy. He felt as if they were in alien territory, and Snabel might leap out from behind a bush or a boulder and open fire with a deadly weapon.

"Grandpa, what *is* this invention he wants so badly?" said Pete, perhaps for the hundredth time since they started the journey.

"It's very important," said Mr. Peck gravely, "and you really are safer, Pete, if you don't know."

They drove on then, past more rock formations, until they came to a prairie dog village. The ground was pocked with holes, and the prairie dogs scooted from one hole to another or sat sunning themselves in their doorways.

It was barely 11:00 a.m. when they finished their

detour through the Badlands. They got back on
the interstate highway and sped eastward. Now the
land was level and the road stretched for miles and
miles in front of them, with scarcely a dip or a
curve. They saw cars ahead and cars behind, but
none were Lincolns. Ben Peck drove fast, over-
taking other cars, staring at the drivers as he
went by.

After a bit Mr. Peck slowed down and let other
drivers pass him. He saw no sign of Edgar Snabel.

"I don't get it," said Peck. "He's not ahead of
us on this road, and I can't see him behind us. He
hasn't passed us and we haven't passed him, but
I'd bet my bottom dollar he's around somewhere.
How does he do it?"

Pete had been keeping watch out of the back
window, and he suddenly stiffened. "Motorcycles!" he announced. "Hey, Grandpa, wouldn't it
be wild if they were the same gang we saw in Crescent City?"

Mr. Peck checked his rearview mirror. "We're
awfully far from Crescent City, unless they're bound
for a thugs' convention somewhere. I understand
those people do have conventions."

The bikers were riding in military formation.
There were two lines of them, and they sat very
straight as they sped along, looking ahead. They
were certainly as ominous as the crew in Crescent

City, and as armored with black leather and nail-heads.

And they were steadily catching up with the Buick.

"Grandpa, can't you go any faster?" said Pete.

"We aren't running from *any*body," said Mr. Peck.

Bob grinned. Mr. Peck certainly had his faults, but he did have courage and determination, and the boys were beginning to believe in his resourcefulness.

"No reason to suppose those guys have anything to do with us," he said now. "Even if they are the ones we saw in Crescent City, they've forgotten us by now."

The boys could hear the roar of the bikes, and they saw the lead riders swerve to the left to overtake the Buick and pass it.

"Uh-oh!" said Pete. "That's the big guy who started to run you down on that pier."

Mr. Peck snorted. "How can you possibly tell? He has so many whiskers he hardly looks human."

The biker turned his head to look at the Buick as he roared past, and it was unfortunate that Mr. Peck looked out at the biker at that moment. Their eyes locked, and the biker's eyes widened and his mouth opened in a shout of surprise. The boys saw him grin. Then the biker shouted to his friends and pointed toward Peck and the boys.

"That did it," said Bob. "We're in for it now."

The motorcycles closed in around the Buick and began to slow down.

Ben Peck raced his engine and the Buick spurted ahead. The bikers in front of the car did not turn aside. They rode stolidly, sitting and staring ahead as if daring Mr. Peck to run them down.

"They're betting I won't hit them, and they're right," said Peck bitterly. He braked and slowed.

He looked to the left. Then he edged over slightly. The biker who was pacing him gave way. He drifted left again, and again the biker gave way. There were angry shouts all around, but then it was too late. The Buick was in the fast lane, and the biker who had not dared to block the lane change was trailing in the rear.

"See that ahead?" Peck nodded toward a cloud of smoke that rose from a pasture beside the highway. Someone must have been burning off dead grass, and since there was almost no wind, the smoke drifted close to the ground, obscuring the road. In seconds they would plunge into that dense cloud—and so would the taunting, angry bikers around them.

"When we hit that smoke, you boys hang on tight," said Ben Peck.

There was no time for more of an explanation. They were in the smoke, and the road was gone. The bikers had disappeared. There was nothing but swirling grayness. Ben Peck rapidly yanked the steering wheel to the left.

They flew off the pavement. For a heartbeat they were airborne. Then they jolted back down to earth and bumped into the ditch in the middle of the divider. For a second Pete thought they would turn over, and he yelled. But they stopped safely, facing back toward the west.

Mr. Peck took a deep breath, shoved the car into first, stamped on the gas, and felt the wheels spin. Then they leaped forward, skidding and bumping up out of the ditch, running along the divider parallel to the westbound lanes. Peck looked over his shoulder as they broke clear of the smoke. The fast lane westbound was clear.

"Here we go!" shouted Mr. Peck. He turned the wheel and they jolted over curbing onto the westbound highway, picked up speed, and were in the clear.

"Grandpa, you're great!" yelled Pete.

"Don't crow too soon," warned Mr. Peck. "It won't take those creeps long to figure out what I did."

There was an exit ramp ahead, and Mr. Peck took it. At the bottom of the ramp he turned onto the frontage road and made for a stand of trees half a mile away.

"Now we'll see," he said. He turned off the road and drove in under the trees and stopped. The Buick was now hidden from traffic on the main road.

"They'll never notice us here," he predicted. "They'll be watching the road ahead of them."

He was breathing more rapidly than usual, but he was grinning as he watched the highway.

It was barely a minute before the bikers roared back into view. They were again riding in their rigid formation, and were obviously scanning the road ahead of them as they sped west.

"A bad breed," said Mr. Peck. "I'm afraid they had some nasty surprises in store for us."

The bikers rumbled down the highway and disappeared in the distance.

Suddenly Jupiter pointed. "Look over there," he said.

A gray Lincoln was traveling east on the freeway. A second after Jupe spoke, it slowed.

"Now if that doesn't beat all," said Ben Peck.

"Hey, it may not be Snabel," said Bob. "It may be somebody else altogether."

"And if it is Snabel, we can just let him get ahead

of us for a change," said Pete.

But the Lincoln didn't go ahead. It braked and rolled up onto the shoulder of the highway and stopped. And it was directly opposite the place where Mr. Peck and the boys sat watching!

12

A Close Call

The Lincoln waited with its parking lights blinking.

"It's homed in on us again!" said Mr. Peck. "Blast! It's Snabel and he knows we're here. But how does he know?"

Through the screen of trees, they saw a patrol car appear on the highway. It pulled onto the shoulder behind the Lincoln and a uniformed man got out. Snabel opened the door of the Lincoln and spoke a few words to the state trooper. Then he and the trooper walked to the front of the Lincoln, and Snabel raised the hood of the car and looked at the engine.

"It's an act," decided Jupe. "He's pretending to be a distressed motorist."

Jupe got out of the Buick. "Okay," he said. "While he's pinned down there on the highway, we'll see just how he does it."

"We will?" said Pete. "How?"

"Mr. Peck said it," Jupe explained. "He homes in on us, and that's exactly right. There has to be some kind of device on this car that sends a signal. He intercepts the signal and he knows where we are—and that's how he's been able to follow us without ever being seen. It's the only way he could do it!"

They all scrambled out then, and Mr. Peck ran to open the trunk of the car. Suitcases were hauled out and dumped open on the ground. Seats were yanked from the back. Jupe felt under the front seats and groped beneath the dashboard.

It was Bob who found the thing at last. He had crawled under the car. It was a plastic box no bigger than a bar of soap, and it was taped to the gas tank.

"We'll fix his wagon!" said Mr. Peck. He picked up a rock.

"No, wait!" Jupe took the thing and stood on tiptoe to put it in the crotch of one of the trees. "We'll keep him waiting and wondering for a while longer," said Jupe.

The Three Investigators repacked the car. Mr.

Peck started the motor, and they were off again. This time they bumped slowly away from the highway and north across a stretch of pastureland.

Bob looked back as they went. The last thing he saw on the highway was Snabel talking with the state trooper, and the trooper staring at the Lincoln and scratching his head in bewilderment.

After a time Mr. Peck found an oiled country road. He turned east and drove through a succession of country villages. Between the villages were long stretches of more pastureland which were sometimes dotted with cattle and horses. At Pierre, South Dakota, they crossed the Missouri River and then there were more small towns and more stretches of pastureland.

They stopped that night at a little bed-and-breakfast inn in a town not fifty miles from the Minnesota state line. There was a locked garage where Mr. Peck could park his car, and their hostess was a smiling and relaxed woman named Mrs. Leonard who talked constantly without ever expecting an answer.

She prepared an excellent supper. The next morning she made them a real farmhand's breakfast, and they were off again through the soft, moist country air.

They kept off the interstate highway most of

the way across Minnesota. But at Rochester they picked it up again and sped on toward La Crosse, Wisconsin. Mr. Peck was jubilant.

"Snabel or no Snabel, we'll see La Crosse," he said. "Pete's grandmother grew up there. It's one of the nicest towns you can imagine."

"Now that we've gotten rid of that gadget Snabel stuck us with, we shouldn't have to worry," Pete pointed out.

"That Snabel sure is a sneaky one," said Mr. Peck. "He must have come prepared for some professional-type spying. Probably been planting bugs around my place for years. No wonder he knows so many things that are none of his business."

Jupiter might once have taken this sort of statement with several grains of salt. Now he was a firm believer. Snabel definitely *was* following them across the country—and it seemed he wanted to get hold of Mr. Peck's invention, whatever it might be.

And wherever it might be. Jupe wondered. They had searched the car but seen no sign of an unusual invention. Was Mr. Peck carrying it in his pocket? Or in his head? How could Snabel steal it if Mr. Peck carried it in his head?

And why had Snabel met with that man in Monterey? At Fisherman's Wharf there had been that second man—the well-dressed person who had melted away and vanished at the first sign of trouble. This man had not appeared to have any interest in Mr. Peck, however. Why had he come to meet Snabel?

"There it is!" cried Mr. Peck suddenly.

They were on a bridge crossing a river, and Mr. Peck announced that it was the Mississippi. The boys saw green bluffs that loomed above the water and islands richly shaded with trees. There was a town on the far side of the river.

"That's La Crosse," said Mr. Peck. "We'll stay there overnight."

That evening they had dinner at a restaurant right on the riverbank. They watched mud swallows skimming above the water and a heron wading near one of the islands.

"The Mississippi must have looked like this to Mark Twain," said Mr. Peck. "Remember Tom Sawyer hiding out on an island with Huck? It must have been that kind of an island."

"Can we take a ride aboard a sternwheeler?" asked Bob eagerly. "A flier at the motel desk said a boat leaves from downtown La Crosse every couple of hours."

"We'll do it!" declared Mr. Peck.

The next morning at 10:45 they were waiting to board the *La Crosse Queen*. The little boat plied back and forth from the pier at the foot of State

Street to the locks just above La Crosse. Mr. Peck was slightly disappointed to learn that it was powered by a diesel engine rather than a proper old-fashioned steam engine. Pete quickly pointed out that diesels were not likely to blow up and sink the boat, while steam engines had been known to do just that.

"Well, all right," said Mr. Peck, "as long as it's really a sternwheeler."

He and the boys went aboard as soon as they were permitted. They took places on the upper deck and watched other sightseers cross the gangplank from the pier. They also saw joggers sweating their way around the riverside park, and children playing on the grass. And Mr. Peck saw something that filled him with rage.

"Look!" he shouted. "Look! It's th-that other one!"

The boys looked where he pointed. They had left the Buick parked near the pier, and now they saw a man standing behind the car, studying it in a curious way.

Jupe gasped. It was the well-dressed man who had met Snabel on the pier in Monterey!

"It's him, isn't it?" cried Mr. Peck. "It's that other one. Oh, wait till I get my hands on him!"

He dashed to the stairway that led down to the main deck. But other passengers were coming up, and the engine of the *La Crosse Queen* was throbbing. By the time Mr. Peck reached the main deck, the gap between the ship and the pier was widening, and they were under way.

It was more than an hour before the riverboat returned to the pier. Mr. Peck and the Three Investigators were the first ones off the boat. They ran to the Buick.

The car was undamaged. There was no sign that anyone had tampered with it. Pete crawled underneath to inspect it from the bottom. Bob and Jupe took the suitcases out of the trunk and examined the rear. Mr. Peck felt under the dashboard and peered into the engine.

"Nothing!" said Mr. Peck. "Now what in tarnation was that one doing? And how did they find us again? After we got rid of that thing they taped to the gas tank, how did they find us?"

"Maybe they lay in wait," said Bob.

The others looked puzzled.

"What I mean is, if I really wanted to find somebody who's crossing the country, I'd go to the places where tourists always go, and I'd wait. In La Crosse, I'd watch the sternwheeler to see if the guy I wanted was going to take a ride."

Mr. Peck nodded. "Yes. That could be it. You're a bright boy, Bob. You're all bright boys."

"Maybe we should beat it out of here," said Bob, "and from now on, stay away from the tourist traps. When we kept off the main highway, there wasn't any trouble."

"Okay," said Mr. Peck. "We'll get on quickly, and when we get to New York it will be all over. Snabel will be out of luck, and out of chances."

They were out of La Crosse within fifteen minutes and speeding southeast on a series of smaller state routes. That night they stayed on the outskirts of Rockford, Illinois.

The next morning they went into Chicago and Mr. Peck treated the boys to a quick trip down Lake Shore Drive, past luxury homes and apartment buildings that faced Lake Michigan. "Now you can say you've been there," announced Mr. Peck. They had lunch atop one of the city's tall buildings, and then were on their way across Indiana.

They stayed that night in Sturgis, Michigan, just to the north of the interstate through Indiana. Bob left his friends for a brief time and went into a supermarket. The camera shop on the main street of the town was closed, and he was out of film.

He found a counter at one side of the store where the assistant manager sold him two rolls of film. He paid and started for the exit. Suddenly his way was blocked.

The elegant stranger from Monterey was standing in his path.

Bob stared at the man and found himself transfixed. For a moment he could not speak. He could not move.

"You don't have it with you," said the man. His voice was flat, without emotion, like his bland, smooth face. "It's all right. We will get it."

He grasped Bob's arm. "Come along now." A hint of a smile came and went across his face.

Bob tried to pull back, but he could not. The man's grip was like steel. Now the man turned toward the automatic door, and Bob was towed along. The door whooshed open as the two approached. Beyond the door was the parking lot, and beyond that . . .

Wild thoughts shot through Bob's mind, one after the other. The well-dressed stranger had to be a partner of Mr. Snabel's. Together they would hold Bob for ransom until they got what they had wanted all along—Mr. Peck's invention. What if the stubborn old man refused to hand it over? What if . . . ?

Bob shouted. He dug in his heels. There was a water cooler near the door, and he threw himself at it and grabbed it and hung on—hung on in spite of the fact that he had hold of the button that turned on the water. Water spouted over his face and ran down his neck and wet his shirt, but he kept holding on and yelling.

"Now see here, son," said the stranger. "You've got to stop that."

The man kept his voice firm and low and determined. He sounded like a parent correcting a disobedient child.

The assistant manager was there all of a sudden. "Trouble?" he said.

"Not really," said the stranger. He still held fast to Bob with one hand, and with the other he tried to untangle him from the water cooler. "My boy's been . . . uh . . . he's been up to—"

"Kidnapper!" croaked Bob. He shifted so that the water no longer spurted on him. "Arsonist! Crook! Get the cops, mister! This guy isn't my dad. I never saw him before in my life!"

A small crowd gathered. There were four or five shoppers with their carts. There was a young stock clerk in a red jacket.

"Charlie," said the assistant manager to the clerk, "just step to the phone and call Henry Parsons to come from the sheriff's office, will you? We'll let him see about this."

"Ridiculous!" snapped the elegant stranger. "I mean, I don't want . . . don't want the police brought into this. The boy doesn't have a record, and if I can nip this in the bud, he won't have to have one."

The man lowered his voice. "He's been experimenting with pot and . . . and maybe something a little heavier, and I want to take care of it before—"

"This guy is not my dad!" insisted Bob. "He doesn't even know my name!"

The assistant manager looked questioningly at the stranger.

"Ask him!" urged Bob. "Make him tell you my name. I'll bet he can't do it."

The stranger only smiled in his smooth way. "My son Ralph is extremely stubborn. It's a family trait, I'm afraid."

Bob let go of the water cooler. He took his wallet out of his pocket and handed it to the market man. "My student identification card is there," he said. "It's got my picture on it."

And as the assistant manager opened the wallet, the elegant stranger turned and disappeared through the exit.

13

Pete Rides High

Bob sat in a dank little room behind the dairy section of the supermarket, trying to answer the deputy sheriff's questions.

It was not easy.

"But why would anyone follow you across the country?" said the officer.

"Mr. Peck says it's because he has an invention these guys want to get," said Bob. "I guess it must be true."

Bob then explained that Mr. Peck was his friend's grandfather. Then he had to describe those of Mr. Peck's inventions he knew about and how the elderly inventor had refused to tell the boys about the all-important one he was going to sell in New York.

"He thinks something might happen to us if we know too much," said Bob.

"It almost happened anyway," said the officer.

Bob nodded, and he gratefully accepted a ride with the deputy back to the motel where he had left Jupiter and Pete and Mr. Peck.

Mr. Peck raged when he learned what had happened, and although he absolutely refused to discuss his invention with the officer, he gladly recounted the tale of the pursuit from Rocky Beach. He left nothing out—not the fire in the motel in Coeur d'Alene or the tracking device fastened to the gas tank or the fact that the stranger from Monterey had prowled around their car in La Crosse.

When Mr. Peck started his recital, the officer was polite and attentive. By the time he finished, the deputy's face was a study in disbelief.

"I see," he said. "Is that all?"

"Isn't that enough?" snapped Mr. Peck.

"It certainly is," said the officer.

Jupiter remembered the license number of the car he had seen near Mount St. Helens, and he gave it to the officer. The officer wrote it down and had Mr. Peck sign the report along with Bob. Then the deputy left, looking uncomfortable.

"They'll never get those two," said Mr. Peck. "They're long gone by now."

No one contradicted him.

Later that evening, when the boys were bedded down for the night, Jupe said, "Something doesn't make sense."

Pete groaned, ready for sleep.

"What do you mean, Jupe?" Bob said.

"Why would Snabel's colleague want to kidnap you, Bob?"

"To get Mr. Peck's invention," Bob answered.

"No, I mean why *you* in particular rather than Mr. Peck or one of us," Jupe said.

"Gee, I don't know," said Bob. "Maybe because I was alone."

"Maybe it's his animal magnetism," Pete put in.

Ignoring him, Jupe went on thoughtfully, "And he said, 'You don't have it with you.' We're assuming that 'it' is Mr. Peck's invention because that's what has been on our minds. But in fact, 'it' could be anything."

"Jupe," Bob pleaded, "can we go over this tomorrow? I've had enough for one day."

"Me too," Pete said. "This is supposed to be our vacation, after all."

Jupe looked grumpy but said, "All right."

They wished each other good night and before long the only sound was the pulsing rumble of the snores next door.

* * *

The next morning the Investigators and Mr. Peck were off before dawn, and now their journey had really become a flight. They decided to forget about traveling by the side roads. No matter what sort of road they used, their pursuers seemed able to find them. And so they used the interstate, where at least there was plenty of traffic. If Snabel and his companion tried anything violent—if they tried to force the Buick off the road, for example—Mr. Peck and the boys could get help.

They sped on and on through Indiana and Ohio. By dusk Mr. Peck was stiff and cranky and exhausted. He was fuming at the thought that he was letting Snabel stampede him. They were in Pennsylvania when he rebelled completely, shot down an off-ramp, and checked into a motel not two hundred yards from the interstate.

"You boys go have a swim for yourselves, or watch television or something," he said. "I'm going to get gas. I'll be right back."

"We'll go with you, Grandpa," said Pete quickly.

"I do not need a guardian yet!" snapped Ben Peck. "There's a gas station down that road. I'll be right back."

He went off, in no mood to be contradicted. The boys turned on the television set in their room but were too jumpy to watch. They waited.

Twenty minutes ticked by, and then half an hour.

"Something's happened to him," said Pete.

Jupiter was pacing and Bob was looking out the window. They were on the outskirts of a small city, and Bob could see its lights beyond the trees.

"Maybe he thought of something he wanted to get at a store, and he went on into town," said Bob.

"Or he didn't like the prices at the gas station down the road, so he went to find another," said Jupe.

Another fifteen minutes passed and the Three Investigators could not wait any longer. They put on their jackets and started down the road.

Mr. Peck was not at the nearest filling station. The attendant there had not seen him. "And I'd notice a car from California," he said. "Even here close to the interstate, we don't get many of those."

The boys continued on, and the darkness deepened. Mr. Peck was not at the second filling station they came to. The third station was on a corner. The attendant there was hardly older than the boys and he did remember an elderly man with a Buick.

"Half an hour ago," said the boy. "Had to be at least that long. The old guy filled the tank and I checked the oil and water for him, and the tires."

"You remember which way he went when he left here?" said Pete eagerly.

"Back the way he came," said the boy. He waved

in the direction of the motel. "I don't know whether he kept on going or not because at that point a couple of guys came in on motorcycles and I got kind of busy."

"Motorcycles?" said Pete quickly.

Jupe felt a shiver of foreboding. "How many bikers were there?" he asked.

"Two of them. Why?" said the boy.

"We . . . we had some trouble with some bikers farther west," said Jupiter. "These probably aren't the same ones, but did you notice which way they went?"

"They went back that way too," said the attendant. "Same as the old guy. They asked me where'd be a good place to camp for the night. I told them the picnic grounds at Parson's Woods. Hey, listen, if you think something's happened to the old man and they had something to do with it I could . . . I could call the cops."

The boys hesitated. Then Pete thought of his grandfather's hair-trigger temper. Mr. Peck had been on the point of exploding that evening. If he felt that the boys were worrying needlessly, he really would be furious.

"Thanks," said Pete. "We'll . . . we'll let you know."

"How do we get to this picnic place?" asked Bob.

The attendant assured the boys that it was hardly half a mile away. He took a blank work order from the office and drew a map for them on the back of the paper. The Investigators thanked him and started back up the street toward the interstate. Bob clutched the smudgy map in his hand.

Before they reached the motel where they were staying, there was a road that went off to the left. Following the map, the boys took this and found themselves on a lane where there were no houses or stores, and only an occasional streetlight. Then there were no streetlights at all, only the pale glow of the rising moon.

But after a time there was a light. Someone had built a fire in a clearing off to the left of the road. The Investigators could see two men moving about in the flickering light. The boys walked on quietly and soon saw the Buick. It had been driven up off the road and parked not far from the fire. Beyond the car and beyond the fire sat Mr. Peck. He sat hunched on a picnic bench with his back to a wooden table. He was watching the two men who moved about the fire between him and the Buick. The old man's expression was stony.

"It's those same bikers," whispered Pete. "They've got Grandpa!"

"Shhh!" warned Jupiter.

An unpaved path led from the road to the picnic ground. The boys stole along this until Bob almost fell over the two motorcycles that had been left there. The Investigators stopped then and crouched beside the bikes, listening.

The voices near the campfire were loud with contempt.

"You ain't seen nothin' yet, old man!" said one biker. "We'll take you for a ride you won't never forget."

The speaker swigged from a can, then crumpled it in one hand and tossed it over his shoulder. Fumbling in a paper bag on the ground, he came up with another can. He drank greedily, belched, and wiped his mouth with his sleeve.

Mr. Peck made a disgusted sound and looked away.

"Hey, you look at me when I'm talkin' to you!" shouted the biker.

Pete jumped. Jupe caught his arm and held on.

"You ever been speedin' up and over the hills, old timer, off the roads where there ain't nobody ever rode before?" said the first biker.

The second man laughed. "Man, that's livin'! You're gonna love it, old man—if it don't kill you!"

They both laughed.

Jupe had let go of Pete's arm, and he suddenly realized that Pete was not there beside him. He had slipped off into the darkness. Jupe's mouth went dry with fright.

But then Pete was back. He leaned close to Jupe

and beckoned to Bob to listen. "Hey, those guys left the keys in their bikes, and Grandpa's keys were in the car too," he whispered. He held up a set of keys, and then a second set, and then a third.

"They're not going to take Grandpa anywhere!" he whispered fiercely. "Take the keys and beat it back to that filling station and call the cops. I'll stay here, and if they try to hurt Grandpa, I'll . . . I'll . . ."

He stopped, unsure how to finish the threat.

Jupe grinned. A beautiful, beautiful idea had just come to him.

Jupe sat still for a second or two, turning his idea over and over in his mind. He could find very little fault with it. It should work. It should enable them to get Mr. Peck out of there safe and sound.

"Listen!" Jupe whispered to Pete. "You rode old Charlie Fisher's bike once or twice, didn't you?"

Jupe was referring to one of Rocky Beach's town characters. Charlie Fisher was an elderly man who supported himself by doing yard work. He owned a decrepit motorcycle and he liked young people, and sometimes, when he trusted a kid especially well—like Pete—he let that kid try riding the motorcycle.

But Charlie's ancient bike and the powerful machines that belonged to the two bikers were as different as day and night.

Pete frowned at Jupe. "You want me to ride one of those bikes out of here?" he whispered. "You crazy or something?"

"Maybe," said Jupe. "Maybe not."

Then he told the rest of his plan.

It was a good plan, and Pete admired it. But he felt that there was a flaw. If it didn't work—if Pete were not as coordinated on a motorcycle as he hoped—the bikers would probably beat him up. Unless Bob and Jupe could outfight them, which was highly doubtful.

On the other hand, unless Pete and his friends acted quickly, the bikers would give Mr. Peck a rough time. Pete could not let that happen.

"Okay," said Pete. "Let's do it!"

The boys crept to the Buick. Slowly and quietly they opened the trunk and got out some tools. Then they set to work.

The bikers had swilled many cans of beer by now. Their voices were thick and their movements were clumsy. Pete guessed they would not have noticed any noise made by the Investigators, but the boys were taking no chances. They worked quietly and mostly by feel. It did not take long, once they got the hang of the tools.

"Thank goodness there's only two of them," said Jupe under his breath. "We'd never be able to pull this off if the whole gang were here."

Slowly, not making a sound, Jupe slid the keys back into the ignition of the first bike. Then he handed the second set of keys to Pete, who stood by the other bike.

The bike was huge. Pete was the tallest of the Three Investigators, and also the strongest. Yet he could barely straddle the motorcycle and touch the ground with his feet. He got the bike off its stand, however, put the key in the ignition, and took a deep breath. Then he put his foot against the starter, turned the key, and kicked back.

The bike roared like an angry animal, and then it went dead.

Pete felt weak with terror. The bikers shouted and scrambled to their feet.

Pete kicked the starter again.

Again the bike roared. This time it did not die. Pete leaned forward and went with it as the bike skidded and jolted away like a bucking horse. The bike jounced into a ditch and then flew up and out onto the road. Pete yelled and kept yelling, but he hung on.

The bikers piled onto the other bike, one behind the other, and the front man kicked the starter and they were off. Unlike Pete, they were in control—for a moment. Suddenly there was a shout and a curse and the men were tumbling in the dirt as the front wheel came off.

The bikers scrambled to get out of the way of the careening, one-wheeled monster that was tearing up the ground, spinning in an erratic circle.

Jupiter and Bob raced to Mr. Peck. Each of them grabbed an arm and hustled the old man toward the Buick. For a second he didn't comprehend what was happening, but then he understood. He ran for his life and snatched open the door of the Buick. The boys scooted in on the passenger side, tossed the car keys to Mr. Peck, and before they got the door closed the car was moving. Mr. Peck swung it in a wide U-turn that flattened half a dozen bushes. Narrowly missing a tree, he tore past the two stunned bikers. Then the car was out in the clear.

A quarter of a mile down the road Mr. Peck slowed. The boys looked back.

The bikers were out in the road, raging and waving their arms.

Jupe and Bob laughed.

14

The Deadly Secret

Pete limped back to the hotel half an hour later. He was wet and dirty, but he was jubilant.

"I ran the bike into a pond," he reported. "I dropped the keys in a mailbox. That'll pin those guys down for a while.

"Grandpa, what happened anyway?" Pete asked. "How'd you get into such a mess?"

Mr. Peck looked a little embarrassed. "Well, Pete, those apes caught me by surprise. I did get gas at a filling station as I told you I would. Then I pulled off on that side road to check whether Snabel or his cohort had attached a new tracking device to the gas tank. While I was looking under the car, those cretins zoomed up out of nowhere and threatened to break all my bones if I didn't do

124

what they said. One of them got in the car and made me drive to that picnic place."

Jupiter looked grave. "You were in a lot of danger, you know. You were lucky to escape unharmed."

"Oh, you needn't fret about me, Jupe," said the old man, perking up. "I was waiting for those cavemen to drink themselves into a stupor and then they'd see. I still have a few tricks up my sleeve."

Pete wasn't sure what his grandfather was referring to but he decided he'd rather not find out.

"Did you call the cops?" Pete said.

"I'm having nothing to do with officialdom on this one," said Mr. Peck. "I don't want to lose any more time trying to explain myself to moronic law officers. We are getting out of town, and we are heading west."

"West?" said Pete.

"West. The bikers will never expect us to go that way. Also Snabel and his pal—if they are watching—will never expect us to go that way. We will find some nice little city somewhere west of here and we will find a car dealer. We will trade in the Buick for another car and then we will go our way in peace. It's the Buick that's given us away every time. Snabel knows it. His pal knows it. The bikers know it. It's got to go."

Pete gazed at his grandfather with admiration. "Hey! Pretty sharp!"

"So are you!" said Mr. Peck. "All right, boys. Get your things together. And mine too. I'm going to check out."

The color was high in the old gentleman's cheeks now, and his eyes sparkled. "I'll get the car," he said, "and bring it around to the side door—the one near the swimming pool. You meet me there with the bags. And Pete, get some dry clothes on."

Pete was already pulling off his wet shirt, and Bob and Jupe were cramming things into suitcases. Mr. Peck grinned. He was coping with his enemies now, and not simply running from them.

Soon Mr. Peck and the boys were back on the interstate speeding west. It was almost midnight when they pulled off the highway into a town on the border of Ohio and Pennsylvania. The streets were deserted and most of the buildings were dark, but there were lights at the Holiday Inn near the interstate, and the travelers checked in there. They slept through the rest of the night and were up early, and when the Ford agency nearest the motel opened that morning, they were waiting.

Mr. Peck agreed almost without argument to the price the salesman offered him on the Buick. He chose a two-year-old Ford sedan from the used car section of the lot and wrote a check. Then he and the boys waited in the office while long-distance calls were made to verify the fact that the check was good.

It was after noon when Mr. Peck and the boys left the car lot, driving the Ford.

"I think we shook them all," said Mr. Peck, who had been keeping a wary eye out for any sign of Snabel or his companion. He yawned widely and rubbed his eyes. "I'm not as young as I used to be," he said. "I keep forgetting that. What say we stay over here for a day and rest up? The pressure's off now. Snabel will never spot us in this Ford."

The boys were certainly willing. They went back to the Holiday Inn, and Mr. Peck was soon snoring as happily as usual.

The boys swam in the motel pool and played some miniature golf at a nearby course, but they did not wander far. Late in the afternoon they came back to their room. Bob and Pete watched television while Jupe sat near the window and stared out. He was frowning and pulling at his lip, a sure sign that he was doing some heavy thinking. Suddenly he nodded and said, "Of course!"

The other two looked at him. "Of course what?" Bob said.

"It isn't your grandfather's invention that Snabel is interested in," said Jupiter. "It never was."

Pete looked stunned. "You're . . . you're kidding! It has to be. That guy started after us at Custer with a gun. You think he was out to shoot buffalo or something?"

"And what about his pal who tried to grab me in that supermarket?" said Bob.

"He's exactly the one I was thinking about," said Jupiter. He cleared his throat importantly and sat up straight. He was preparing to expound a theory. "What exactly did that man say to you in the supermarket, Bob?"

"He said I was his kid and I was on dope and he wanted to take me away. It was plain enough. He was probably going to hold me for ransom— and the ransom would have been Mr. Peck's invention. Do you suppose it could have something to do with national defense? It seems like a lot more than a smoke bomb."

"I'm not so interested in the explanation he gave the store manager. What was it he said to you before the manager got there?"

"Oh, it was something like . . . like, 'I know you don't have it, so come along,' or, 'You don't have it with you, do you?' Something like that."

"And what didn't you have with you then?" asked Jupiter.

"Well . . . well, Mr. Peck's invention, I suppose. What else?"

"Couldn't it have been something else?" suggested Jupe. "Couldn't it have been something you usually carry that you didn't have with you that evening?"

Bob scowled. "I don't know what that would be, unless—oh, wow! Sure! My camera and the camera case. But what . . . why would that guy care about that?"

Jupiter grinned. "Yes. The camera and the case holding your exposed film. You'd left them behind at the motel, and that's what those two want. I'd bet my life on it!"

Jupe sat back and put the tips of his fingers together so his hands made a little tent. He was smiling. "I don't think Snabel was following us when we first set out on this trip," he said. "Remember how he looked when Mr. Peck pounced on him on the beach at Pismo? He was startled and scared. I believe he was at Pismo for an entirely different reason.

"Let us suppose that our meeting Snabel at Pismo was strictly accidental. Snabel was not really spying when he sneaked around Mr. Peck's house and

watched us leave that first morning. He was only
doing a little neighborly snooping, which was his
custom. Some time after we left, he left too, plan-
ning to drive to Monterey to meet someone there.
We delayed for an hour or so on the road, having
lunch at Santa Barbara. He went directly to Pismo
Beach, where he stopped to rest and stretch his
legs. He walked on the beach, as we did, and when
your grandfather saw him and flew into a temper,
Snabel was at least as surprised as Mr. Peck. Remember his face?

"He got away down the beach and then went
on to Monterey, and that's where the whole situ-
ation changed. Do you remember what happened
at Monterey?"

"Well, we ran into him again on the wharf," said
Pete, "and we saw that other guy—the one who
tried to grab Bob."

"Right. And Snabel was definitely *not* following
us when he arrived at Fisherman's Wharf. He was
making no attempt to keep out of sight. He walked
onto the pier quite openly, looking like any other
tourist."

Jupe covered his eyes with his hand. Bob and
Pete knew that he was remembering the scene
again—replaying it in his remarkable memory, as
one would replay a videotape. Details that did not
seem especially important when the Investigators

had bumped into Snabel on Fisherman's Wharf might now stand out.

"Snabel had his camera that day—a camera just like Bob's—but he didn't try to take any pictures. He just waited with the camera in his hands. Then the second man arrived and Snabel said to him, 'I brought it.'

"Wouldn't that indicate that Snabel was delivering something to the second man? And the second man told him to move, and they walked away from us and stood near the bench where Bob was sitting. Then Snabel recognized us. Remember how pale he got? And Mr. Peck came out of the shop where he had been watching the whole thing. The man who had come to meet Snabel just drifted away. Suddenly he simply wasn't there. Mr. Peck grabbed Snabel and told Snabel he wasn't going to get away with it, and that he had better wise up and forget whatever it was he had planned to do.

"Again Snabel was frightened. He hadn't expected to see Mr. Peck there. Mr. Peck told us we were leaving, and Bob picked up his camera, which had been beside him on the bench, and we left.

"And that's where it all started, because that's where Snabel first tried to come after us. Remember how he chased the car as we drove away, and he shouted?"

Pete nodded, and Bob stared at Jupe.

"Right," Bob said. "But why?"

"Because it wasn't your camera you picked up, Bob," said Jupiter. "It was the one Snabel had brought with him—the one Snabel had put down on the bench when Mr. Peck collared him."

"You mean it's the camera he's after?" Pete said. "But that doesn't make sense. If it was the camera he wanted, why wouldn't he just come up to the door of our motel room in Santa Rosa and knock and say, 'Hey, guys, you've got my camera and I've got yours, and here it is'? Why all this tracking and trailing and kidnapping and stuff?"

"Because if it were just the camera, it wouldn't matter, would it? No one would drive all the way from Monterey to Santa Rosa just for a camera. No one would follow us all the way across the country. It has to be the film that was in the camera. That's what's important to Snabel and the other man, and they don't want us to know about that film."

"Yes," said Bob. "Could be." He got up and dumped his camera bag on the bed. There were nine rolls of film, one of them unused. The rest were exposed and sealed shut to await developing.

"There's got to be a fast photo store somewhere in this town," said Bob. "Let's find it."

They did. It was in a small mall three blocks from the hotel. The Investigators handed over Bob's film to the woman behind the counter, and then they stayed in the mall and wandered from display window to display window until it was time to pick up their prints.

Bob found that he was shaking as he carried the yellow envelopes from the photo store to the parking lot. Pete and Jupe looked over his shoulder while he shuffled through the prints. They saw pictures of Mr. Peck at Mount Rushmore, pictures of the bison at Custer, and pictures of the rock spires in the Badlands. And among all the tourist treasures there was a photograph of an aircraft lifting off a runway.

"I didn't take that," said Bob.

Pete took the print and examined it closely. The aircraft was slender, almost like a needle, and it had swept-back wings. "Looks like a military plane," said Pete. "It sure isn't just another passenger plane."

Bob thumbed through other prints. He saw shots of some sort of installation that looked like a cross between an oil refinery and a grain elevator. There were close-up pictures of drawings and diagrams that had been spread out on a board and then held down with pushpins. There were shots someone had taken of an open notebook—pages of equations and notations that were meaningless to the boys.

Bob was sweating when they finished looking through the pictures. "So that's what he was going to deliver to the second guy," he said. "Th-they could be pictures of military installations, couldn't they? He could be a spy—a real spy—selling classified information to an enemy!"

15

Spy Bait

"The FBI!" cried Mr. Peck. "That's it! We'll call the FBI, and they'll gather up that wretch!"

Pete already had the telephone directory out. "Not here," he said. "No FBI office in this town."

"Did you think there would be?" said Mr. Peck. "We're going to the FBI in New York, and we're going right now. Pack up!"

They did, and they drove through that night and then through the grayness of early morning until at last they plunged into a tunnel that gleamed with white tile and hummed with traffic. Beyond the tunnel was the great city—towering buildings, a tangle of traffic, and taxis jockeying for position outside a massive structure that turned out to be Pennsylvania Station.

Mr. Peck stopped the car across the street from the station while Jupe went inside to look in the telephone book for the address of the FBI. The boys felt keyed up with excitement. The Three Investigators had cooperated with the Rocky Beach police before, but never with the FBI on a case of possible espionage.

By nine thirty Mr. Peck and the boys had found the office and were closeted with a man they assumed was an agent. His name was Anderson. He was a neat person with sandy hair and even, white teeth, a firm handshake, and a calm manner. The calmness stood him in good stead when Mr. Peck started relating the tale of the scoundrel Snabel who was selling military secrets to the enemy. Mr. Peck was so overcome with indignation that he soon sputtered into incoherence.

The FBI man waited politely for Mr. Peck to get himself under control.

"Grandpa, please!" pleaded Pete. "We aren't really sure about a lot of that. Why not just show the pictures?"

"We *are* sure!" cried Mr. Peck. But he slammed the envelope of photographs down on the desk. "These were in Bob's camera—except that it isn't Bob's camera," he declared. "It was switched. That traitor Snabel was peddling these to a foreign agent!"

Mr. Anderson looked at the pictures, and his face remained expressionless.

Jupiter seized the opportunity to take hold of the conversation.

"Mr. Anderson, I'd like to introduce myself and my friends." With that, Jupe took a card out of his pocket and handed it to the agent. Mr. Anderson dutifully read the card, which said:

> ## THE THREE INVESTIGATORS
> "We Investigate Anything"
> ? ? ?
> First Investigator .... Jupiter Jones
> Second Investigator ... Peter Crenshaw
> Records and Research ... Bob Andrews

Mr. Anderson opened his mouth as if to ask a question, but Jupiter plunged on. "I am Jupiter Jones, the head of our detective firm, which is based in Rocky Beach, California. We have investigated mysteries of every description, so we are not unaware of the techniques of detection."

Bob thought he could make out a gleam of amusement in Mr. Anderson's otherwise impassive face as the man carefully laid the boys' card on his desk.

Jupe kept going. "Of course," he said, looking

down a little shyly, "we've never run across anything of such significance. And it's truly a privilege
to be cooperating with the FBI—"

"Get on with it," Pete interrupted impatiently.

Jupe glared at the Second Investigator. Turning
back to the agent, he continued, ". . . on a case that
possibly may affect our national security."

Jupe went on to explain how the cameras were
switched in Monterey.

"That was the beginning of a series of threat-
ening events," said Jupe.

"That crook has been trying to get us ever since!"
cried Mr. Peck.

But then Mr. Peck subsided. Jupe told about the
motel fire in Coeur d'Alene, Idaho, about seeing
Snabel on the trail in Custer State Park, South
Dakota, and finally about the attempt to kidnap
Bob in Michigan.

"No doubt there is a record in Sturgis, Michigan,
of a kidnap attempt several days ago. The supermarket manager called the sheriff there."

The FBI man was silent, waiting to see if Jupe
had more to add. After a moment he nodded. "I
see," he said.

Jupiter sat back, satisfied with his recital. He had
been logical, orderly, precise, and, he was sure,
convincing. Now Mr. Peck leaped to the attack
again.

"That skunk Snabel's got a talent for spying," he said, "and the one with him must be an enemy agent."

The FBI man smiled. "I don't suppose we know which enemy?"

"Does it matter?" demanded Ben Peck.

"Perhaps not," said the government man. He asked them to wait, and he left the room with the photos. He returned after some time and said only that his colleagues were looking into the story and that they would be in touch.

"Where will you be staying in New York?" he asked.

Mr. Peck gave the name of a small hotel on the East Side called the Riverview Plaza and Mr. Anderson wrote it down.

"If they aren't filled up," added Mr. Peck, suddenly doubtful.

"I think we can check on that, if you don't mind waiting another few minutes," said Anderson.

He went out again, and after a few minutes he was back with word that the Riverview Plaza had two rooms for them.

"If you think of anything else, or if you happen to see Mr. Snabel again, please get in touch with me," he said, and he gave them his card.

The boys knew then that their story had been taken seriously—at least seriously enough to merit investigation. Satisfied, they trooped out and went down in the elevator. Mr. Peck drove to the Riverview Plaza. It was an older building which might once have had a view of the river, but which now was completely hemmed in by tall office buildings. An attendant drove the Ford off to a parking lot somewhere. A second attendant carried their bags upstairs to a suite. Its semi-clean windows looked out on a glassy office building in which rows of men and women sat at computer terminals under fluorescent lights.

Jupe found the sight depressing, and he was glad to pull down the blinds and crawl into bed. He closed his eyes and wondered how long it would be before the FBI checked out their story. He wondered what the agents would do about Snabel, and that was the last thing he wondered before he fell asleep.

He dreamed that he was at home in the salvage yard. In the dream he was tunneling through heaps of junk piled around the trailer that served as the headquarters of The Three Investigators. Jupe had to hurry because the telephone was ringing and ringing and ringing.

He woke sweating with anxiety. The telephone in their hotel room really was ringing. Bob got up and lifted the receiver. Jupe watched, dazed and sleepy, and Bob said, "Yes." Then he said, "Yes, of course."

He put down the telephone. "That was Mr. Anderson calling from the lobby," he said. "He's coming up."

The boys scrambled out of bed and Pete ran to wake Mr. Peck. The old man came from his room with his hair mussed and his feet bare just as the FBI knocked at the door.

Mr. Anderson had a second man with him—a man who was taller and somewhat older than he. Mr. Anderson introduced his companion as Agent Friedlander, then sat down in a little straight chair in a corner and let Friedlander take over the conversation.

Mr. Peck had to answer many questions about Ed Snabel. He managed to do this without sputtering too loudly or going off on too many tangents. What he knew about Snabel was very little, when one considered that Snabel and he had been neighbors for several years. He could tell Friedlander only that he understood Snabel worked for some defense industry, that he appeared to have no family or friends, and that he raised orchids for a hobby. About Snabel's associate who had attempted to kidnap Bob he knew absolutely nothing. However, Bob was able to pick out a photograph of Snabel's colleague from twelve pictures that Friedlander showed him.

"Who is he?" said Bob, after he had identified the stranger. "Has he got a record?"

The picture that Friedlander put back in his pocket was not a regular police mug shot. It showed the elegant stranger in an airport or perhaps a train station. He was coming through a gate as if he had just gotten off a plane.

"He's just a man we've been acquainted with in the past," said Agent Friedlander. "You can call him Bartlett. That's one of his many aliases."

Mr. Anderson came forward and opened an attaché case he had brought with him. He took out several rolls of film. The rolls were sealed as if they had been exposed and were ready to be developed.

"Bob, you'd be doing us an enormous favor if you would carry these in your camera bag," said Anderson. "And don't worry if someone steals the bag. This film has useless pictures on it."

Mr. Peck jumped up. "No!" he shouted. "You're setting the boy up—making a clay pigeon out of him. I'm responsible for him on this trip, and I won't have it!"

Mr. Anderson smiled. "No, Mr. Peck," he said. "We aren't making a clay pigeon of him. He already *is* a clay pigeon. Snabel and his associate might still find you. They've already gone to a great deal of trouble for that film. If they finally get their hands on Bob and he can't give them what they want, what do you suppose they'll do?"

Mr. Peck looked stricken. He sat down again. "It's a stakeout, isn't it?" he said. "Like those police shows we see on television. You'll be following Bob, and when Snabel and this Bartlett make a move, you'll nab them."

Friedlander and Anderson did not admit it, but they didn't deny it either. They simply asked Mr. Peck to keep them informed if Peck and the boys decided to leave New York, or if they moved from the hotel. Then the FBI men left.

When the door closed behind them, Bob whooped. "I get to be a counterspy!" he said. "Till now we've been the ones to be hunted, but now we're the hunters."

"You're the bait!" corrected Mr. Peck. He tried to sound dour and sensible, but he was excited too, in spite of himself. He had never dreamed that by the trip's end he would be working with the FBI—to trap his annoying next-door neighbor once and for all!

16

Grandpa Makes the News

"Four days!" lamented Bob. "Four whole frantic days, and there's no sign of them!"

"We've lost them for good," said Pete. "They'll never find us now."

Jupe said nothing. He sat on a stone bench in front of the American Museum of Natural History and watched the pigeons strut on the pavement. He also watched Ben Peck.

The old gentleman was scowling at the traffic that rumbled past. Not once in the last four days had he mentioned the invention that had brought them all to New York. Not once had he spoken of contacting anyone to present his idea. He was wholly, totally involved in the attempt to lure

144

Snabel and his accomplice into the open. Whenever they left the hotel his blue eyes were alert, his
stance was tense, and he kept very close to Bob.

They had guessed that Snabel and Bartlett might
be watching for them at a favorite tourist attrac-
tion—as had happened in La Crosse, Minnesota.
So they decided to make themselves as visible as
they could, and to see everything there was to be
seen in New York City. Bob would carry his camera
bag everywhere and would rummage in the bag
often, tumbling rolls of film around so that on-
lookers would be sure to see that he had several
exposed rolls awaiting developing.

The plan was logical and they followed it to the
point of exhaustion. On their first day of sightseeing they took a boat tour around Manhattan
Island and then visited the United Nations in the
afternoon. Feeling expansive, Grandpa treated the
boys to dinner in an open-air restaurant atop a
nearby hotel. A pianist entertained the diners with
show tunes while they gazed out at the sea of lights
below. The Investigators could feel the energetic
hum of the city.

The next day they were up and out early—this
time to Brooklyn via subway to dare the roller
coaster at Coney Island. After a whirlwind tour of
the nearby Aquarium, Jupiter had his first potato

knish—a turnover stuffed with mashed potatoes.

"Wait till I tell Aunt Mathilda about this," Jupe said, smacking his lips.

Then the tourists continued on to the Statue of Liberty and ended their day having dinner at the top of the World Trade Center. They were so high up, small planes passed beneath them while they were chewing. Pete gulped and didn't know where to look first. They might be clay pigeons, he thought, but this beat anything he'd seen in Rocky Beach.

Undaunted, Mr. Peck and the boys kept the pace up on the third day. They strolled through historic Greenwich Village and stopped for lunch in Chinatown.

After lunch, Mr. Peck read aloud the slip of paper he'd found in his fortune cookie: YOU WILL BE LUCKY IN LOVE TONIGHT #15267. They all laughed. Then it was time to see the Rockettes at Radio City Music Hall. Dinner at Lindy's followed—crowned by their first taste of New York cheesecake. Totally weary, they fell into bed and slept heavily.

On the fourth day, it was the Metropolitan Museum of Art in the morning followed by a stroll through Central Park. They basked in the sun on a park bench and bought souvlaki sandwiches— chunks of lamb in pita bread—from a pushcart.

Now they had just finished a tour of the Museum of Natural History on the other side of the park.

In the course of all this jaunting about, they had noticed that a young man in a tan sweater and gray slacks was often somewhere nearby. If they did not see him, they saw a hefty, ruddy-faced individual who wore a navy blazer.

"FBI men," Bob decided. "I feel a lot safer with them around."

"Bet they'd like to get their hands on Snabel's pal," said Pete. "He's probably a dangerous international spy."

"Stop letting your imagination run away with you," said Mr. Peck. But he added, "Let's hope these FBI men keep their eyes open."

On the morning of that fourth day of sightseeing, Mr. Peck had dragged himself out of bed, stiff and weary, and Pete had protested.

"Grandpa, why don't you stay there and we'll call down for breakfast?" he said. "Let's forget Snabel. He'll never find us."

"He might," said Mr. Peck, "and I don't aim to take a chance on missing it. Not on your life."

Jupe had grinned, admiring the old man's persistence.

"Something will happen today," Mr. Peck said. "I feel it in my bones."

And so here they were outside the museum, and

now it was late afternoon. But nothing had happened. The man in the tan sweater was nowhere around. The chubbier man in the blue blazer stood at the curb eating an ice cream sandwich that he had bought from a street vendor. He looked bored.

"We're not noticeable enough," said Pete. "This is a big city and Snabel doesn't know where to find us. We need to do something really far out, like climbing up the outside of the Empire State Building or swimming across the Hudson River. That would get us noticed. If we got on television, Snabel couldn't help spotting us."

"Your mother would have my head," said Mr. Peck.

"Well, sure," said Pete, "but everything has its price."

A slow, happy smile spread across Jupe's face. "Television!" he said softly.

"Huh?" said Bob.

"Uh-oh," Pete groaned. "You've got a bright idea. Nothing too strenuous, Jupe, okay? I was only kidding about the Empire State Building."

"It shouldn't be too obvious," said Jupiter. "If we could get on a quiz show, perhaps. Or a newscast of some important event."

"How about a hotel opening?" said Bob. "I read in the paper that there's a new hotel opening in

New York. It's called the New Windsor. It's getting a lot of attention because it was built on the site of an old hotel that burned down a couple of years ago. A lot of literary people used to stay at the old place when they were in town. There's going to be a big party and there's a chance that the governor will come."

"When is the opening?" said Jupe.

"Tomorrow night," Bob answered him. "If the governor comes, there should be TV coverage."

Jupe nodded. "And the FBI should be able to arrange an invitation for us," he said. "If we can move into the hotel instead of just going to the party, so much the better. Snabel and Bartlett will know where to find us."

Jupe rose and went right up to the man in the blue blazer.

"Is there a possibility that the FBI could arrange for us to attend the opening of the New Windsor tomorrow night?" he said.

The man in the blue blazer was so startled at being addressed by the boy that he dropped his ice cream sandwich.

"There's sure to be coverage of the event on the news shows," said Jupiter. He ignored the ice cream, which had splashed on the man's shoes. "If we are interviewed by a newscaster, perhaps one of us can say we're staying at the hotel. Then Edgar Snabel will know where to find us. And you can stop shadowing us all around New York."

The FBI agent had by then recovered his composure. He drew a breath and started to say that he didn't know what Jupe was talking about. Then he stopped himself and nodded. "We'll let you know," he said, and walked away down the street.

Jupe went back to his friends. "We'll be hearing from him," he told them.

"Meantime he leaves us here alone and unprotected," said Mr. Peck.

"Grandpa, don't act helpless," scolded Pete. "You're about as unprotected as a Sherman tank. That guy Snabel's going to have big trouble if he ever does catch up with you."

This made Mr. Peck feel much cheerier, and he insisted that they take a cab back to the Riverview Plaza.

The telephone rang later that evening. Mr. Peck answered. It was Mr. Anderson, who suggested that they pack in anticipation of the next day's move to the New Windsor.

"And do you and the boys have dark suits or blazers?" Mr. Anderson asked. "If you're going to be on television, you want to look as if you came to New York expecting to go to a swank party."

"Oh!" said Mr. Peck. He was taken aback.

"Don't worry about it," said Anderson. "We'll get some things for you."

The New Windsor was barely finished. The cavernous new lobby smelled of paint and shellac. A room service waiter that Bob met on the elevator was finding his way around with the help of a little printed floor plan. The suite assigned to Mr. Peck and the boys was smaller than their rooms at the Riverview, but it was on the thirty-second floor, and they could see the East River from Mr. Peck's bedroom.

When Mr. Peck and the boys moved in about five, the TV men were setting up their equipment in the lobby. When the Californians came down at 6:45, wearing the neat blue blazers the FBI had provided, the place was a blaze of lights. Mr. Anderson was waiting near the message desk. He took them in tow and introduced them to the newscaster who would cover the gala evening for the television station.

The newsman was tall and handsome, with very white teeth and perfectly arranged hair. He shook hands with Mr. Peck while looking past the old gentleman's left ear. Then he stepped around Ben Peck and greeted a woman who had just come in through the revolving door. The woman wore a jacket that had glittery sequins and bits of mirror fastened to it.

Then the red light on the TV camera went on. A man who stood on the sidelines with earphones signaled to the newscaster. The newscaster announced that he was in the lobby of the New Windsor, and that Mrs. Jasper Harrison Wheatly was with him. Mrs. Wheatly had flown all the way from Rome to attend the gala opening of the New Windsor, said the newsman.

The man did not explain why Mrs. Wheatly might be important; the boys supposed that everyone knew why, even if they did not. Her smile was so forced that Pete thought her face might crack. She said a few words, then swept on through the lobby.

Suddenly the announcer was bearing down on Ben Peck and the boys. His hand was out in a welcoming gesture, and the camera with the red light was pointed their way. "And here's Mr. Bennington Peck!" cried the newscaster, as if he was surprised by the coincidence. "A very special guest—and one who has come all the way across the United States just to attend this event."

Ben Peck grinned broadly at the camera. He took hold of the newsman's hand and did not release it again—not before telling the television audience that he and his wife, rest her soul, used to come to the old Westmore Hotel when it stood there. "On our honeymoon . . ." said Mr. Peck.

"The Windsor," said the newscaster. "Yes."

He was trying to get his hand away from Mr. Peck, and he was not succeeding.

"Like I said, the Windsor," boomed Mr. Peck. "We visited often." He stood a little taller. "Struck me all of a heap when the old Westchester burned, but this new one is great. Kind of damp but that'll wear off soon as they get some heat up. The boys and I"—at this point the camera swerved to take in the smiling faces of Jupe, Bob, and Pete—"are enjoying every bit of it, and we're going to stay over at least till the end of the week. Biggest thrill we've had since we rode the Cyclone roller coaster out at Coney Isand."

The announcer managed to wrestle himself free at this point. He backed off, still smiling his professional smile. He thanked Mr. Peck and the boys, and it was over.

Mr. Peck tottered away, wiping his brow with his handkerchief. "Was I all right?" he asked. "What did I say?"

"You were great, Grandpa!" Pete applauded. "You said all the right things—and you said them good and loud!"

"Fine!" said Mr. Peck. "Just so that skunk Snabel knows where to find us."

He and the Three Investigators then made for a Scandinavian restaurant in the Citicorp building to have a bite, since they had not been asked to the grand dinner and reception that was taking place on the roof garden. And if Mr. Peck noticed Mr. Anderson chuckling as he watched them cross the lobby, the old man gave no sign. He had done his job.

How long would it be before Snabel found them?

17

Trapped!

The boys had almost finished their breakfast the next morning when Mr. Peck came into the hotel coffee shop. He had been up until midnight to watch his interview on the late news and then again on the late-late news. When he sat down beside Pete he reported with delight that he had also made the morning news.

He beamed at other patrons in the restaurant, as if he expected to sign autographs for an admiring public. The waiter scurried up with a menu but he did not seem to recognize Mr. Peck. Mr. Peck glared at him.

"Coffee," said Mr. Peck. "Pancakes. Two eggs over easy, and bacon."

"Grandpa, your cholesterol!" said Pete.

"You let me worry about my arteries," snapped his grandfather. "We're going to have a big day and I need my strength."

But after breakfast the big day did not materialize immediately. The Three Investigators arranged themselves in the hotel lobby, and Bob was careful to fiddle with his camera and his camera bag. The government man in the blue blazer loitered in the gift shop, and the one in the tan sweater browsed through the magazines at the news counter.

"Okay, Snabel, we're ready," muttered Mr. Peck.

But nothing happened. The half-hours and the hours ticked by.

By eleven, Mr. Peck had begun to seethe. By eleven thirty, he had come to a full boil.

"Ridiculous!" he said at last. "We could sit here all year. That stupid dolt didn't see the interview! Ignoramus! He doesn't even keep up with the news!"

Then he smiled cunningly. "There's a double header at Yankee Stadium this afternoon," he said. "What say we go?"

"Grandpa, we might ruin everything," said Pete. "If Snabel and his pal did see the interview, they'll look for us here."

"Or just outside," said Mr. Peck. "We're making a mistake sitting here. We have to go out and give them a chance to come sneaking after us like the snakes they are."

"I don't think we have to worry about missing them," said Jupe. "If they get here and we're not here, they'll wait. Or they'll come back. They've chased us across the country to retrieve that film; they're not going to give up now."

So it was settled. Mr. Peck gathered his troops and asked at the message desk what subway train they should take for Yankee Stadium.

It was noon when Mr. Peck and the boys set out for the subway station two blocks from the hotel. The government men who watched over them trailed half a block behind. When they reached the subway platform, Mr. Peck and the boys let a train go by so that the agents could catch up. They rode up to the Bronx ball park with the government men at one end of the subway car and the boys at the other end. Mr. Peck wandered contentedly back and forth, looking at the graffiti.

At the stadium they pretended to be New Yorkers, and they rooted for the Yankees. They felt a comfortable satisfaction when the first game ended with the Yankees ahead by one run.

The boys and Mr. Peck enjoyed hot dogs slathered with mustard and sauerkraut for supper. Then they settled down to enjoy the second game. This time the visiting team outhit the Yankees, which brought forth a torrent of boos, whistles, and Bronx cheers from the loyal fans. Mr. Peck and the boys joined in for the sheer fun of it. Even though the Bronx Bombers lost the second game, Mr. Peck and his crew felt exhilarated as they rose to leave.

The spectators jammed the exits getting out of the stadium, and the boys and Mr. Peck shuffled along elbow to elbow with thousands of others, and at last reached the subway station. The tracks were not underground here, but instead were elevated. In spite of the crowd that jostled him, Mr. Peck enjoyed the evening breeze.

When a train rumbled in bound for Manhattan, Mr. Peck and the boys were swept aboard by the mob of baseball fans. The doors slid shut and the train started out of the station, and only then did Pete see the government man in the tan sweater. He was hemmed in by a crowd that had just surged onto the platform, and he was looking wildly into the cars as they passed. For an instant he and Pete stared into each other's eyes. Then the train picked up speed, and the station and the FBI man were left behind.

Pete was wedged in between a beefy fellow in a plaid sports coat and a teenage boy who was balancing himself without holding on to anything, and who ate peanuts nonstop. Pete wriggled away from the munching boy and got closer to Jupiter, who was hanging from a metal handstrap.

"We lost our bodyguards," Pete said to Jupe. "I saw the one in the tan sweater on the platform as the train pulled out."

"Bodyguard?" echoed a skinny woman in a violet-colored turban. She was jammed in close to Jupe, but she spoke loudly enough to be heard in the next county. "You got a bodyguard? Big deal! What you got that's worth guardin'?"

The woman cackled as if she had said something terribly witty. Several other passengers chuckled and glanced at Pete.

Jupe suddenly sparkled with mischief. "Don't worry," he said to Pete. "You don't need that guy hanging around you. The incubation period was supposed to be up yesterday."

The skinny woman stiffened. She was suddenly wary. "Incubation period?" she shrilled. "What incubation period? You got something catchin'?"

"No, I don't!" said Pete quickly. "Hey, he's only kidding."

The denial only made the woman more suspicious. She backed off, and at the next stop she left the train.

Other people got off too as the train rattled and

swayed toward Manhattan. Soon Mr. Peck and Bob were able to join Pete and Jupe in the clear space in the center of the car.

"Pete saw the government man on the platform," said Jupe to Mr. Peck. "He missed the train. We're on our own."

"That's nothing new," said Ben Peck. "Doesn't seem to matter anyway. If Snabel and company are anywhere around, they're sure being quiet about it."

Which was true. The boys could see the whole length of the subway car now. No passenger even remotely resembled Snabel or his associate.

They left the train at Forty-second Street. Mr. Peck spotted a tunnel that would let them out of the station two blocks closer to their hotel. The tunnel looked dark and uninviting. The boys looked at each other questioningly, shrugged, and followed the old man, who had already started ahead. Halfway down the tunnel they heard the call.

"Ben Peck!" someone shouted.

The tunnel was completely deserted except for one other person—a man who came toward them smiling. He seemed shorter than they remembered, and perhaps stouter, for he was wearing a raincoat that fell in folds from his shoulders.

"Snabel!" cried Mr. Peck.

"Good to see you again," said Snabel. "It's been too long."

The tunnel was so quiet that the boys could hear water dripping somewhere in it.

Then someone spoke behind the boys. "I'll have the camera bag, if you please," said the voice.

It was the man they had seen in Monterey. He had a gun and it was pointed at Bob.

Bob quickly handed over his camera bag.

The elegant stranger looked quickly into the bag to make sure the rolls of film were there. He nodded to Snabel. "Okay," he said to Mr. Peck and the Investigators. "Inside. All of you."

He motioned with his gun to a door in the wall of the tunnel. Snabel had pried off the padlock that secured it. Inside was a damp little closet full of brooms, sponges, and jugs of disinfectant.

"In there," said the man with the gun.

They went in and the door was closed on them. Something was shoved into the hasp outside to secure the door. And footsteps retreated.

"Help!" cried Pete. "Get us out of here!"

18

No Exit for a Traitor

After what seemed like a long time, the token booth attendant released Mr. Peck and the boys. A passerby had heard muffled pounding and cries coming from the closet and had reported it to the attendant. He had brought a transit patrolman with him. When the patrolman tried to question Mr. Peck, Mr. Peck told the man to take a walk. He then marched up the stairs and back to the hotel and called Mr. Anderson.

Mr. Anderson came right over. He seemed quite calm.

This infuriated Mr. Peck still more. "So this is what we get for our taxes!" cried Mr. Peck. "We put our lives on the line. We want to help you catch a pair of dangerous spies. When they take the bait, where are you? Asleep at the switch, that's where!"

"You're positively right, Mr. Peck," said Mr. Anderson.

Mr. Peck then reviewed the events of the day. He spent some time describing his incarceration in a smelly, airless closet with a lot of wet push brooms.

"An outrage!" he shouted, finishing the tale.

"It is indeed," said Mr. Anderson. "It should never have happened."

Mr. Peck found that suddenly he was calmer. He sat down, and Mr. Anderson went on. "Our agents are watching all means of egress from New York City—airports, train stations, bus stations, tunnels, bridges, the works. We have a good chance of catching the two men if they try to leave town."

"And if they don't?" said Ben Peck. "Are we supposed to keep hanging around like sitting ducks?"

"Not at all," said the agent. "This case is over as far as you and the boys are concerned. Those two men won't bother you anymore. Snabel is no longer involved now that his film's been delivered. And when his contact finds the film is a dummy, he'll know that we have the photos he was after. So he's lost and we've won, and no real harm has been done."

"There are a couple of spies still walking around loose," snapped Ben Peck. "I'd say that was harmful."

Mr. Anderson smiled. "Edgar Snabel won't spy again," he said, "because he won't have a chance. You exposed him, Mr. Peck, and you can be proud of that. He can't apply for work in any defense industry without being fingerprinted. If he's crazy enough to apply under an assumed name, we'll have him. But he probably won't even try. He'll fade out of sight, now that we're on to him, and will try to build a new identity in another state."

"But what about that creep who was with him? That Bartlett?" demanded Mr. Peck. "Suppose he tried something else?"

"If we don't catch him, he probably will," said Mr. Anderson. "But we're looking for him—hard. Meanwhile, Mr. Peck—boys—we are thankful for the help you've given us. Please don't think it's a small thing, or unimportant. It isn't."

Mr. Anderson left, and there was a feeling of unease after the door closed on him.

"Rats!" said Pete.

Jupiter nodded solemnly. "It's like trying to sleep in an unmade bed," he said. "You want to get up and straighten the covers."

There seemed no way the Three Investigators could do this. They could think of no possible way of locating Snabel or the elegant Bartlett. They tried to settle down and enjoy what was left of their stay in New York, and Mr. Peck turned his attention to the invention that had prompted him to take the trip in the first place.

The morning after the jaunt to Yankee Stadium, Mr. Peck went out and was gone all day. When he returned to the hotel in the early evening, he announced mysteriously that he had seen his "contacts" and that things appeared to be "moving along."

He then arranged to have the Ford checked and lubed in anticipation of the long trip home.

For the next few days Mr. Peck disappeared early and returned to the hotel late and the boys were left on their own. They went to see a renovated aircraft carrier moored in the Hudson River, visited the Hayden Planetarium, ate cannolis in Little Italy, rode the overhead tramway to Roosevelt Island, took a tour of Rockefeller Center, and shopped for souvenirs. On the fourth day after the boys' disappointing encounter with Snabel, they saw the woman with the orchid.

It was at the corner of Sixth Avenue and Thirtieth Street that the lady passed them. She had the orchid in a pot, and it was a beauty, with three spikes of waxy green and brown flowers.

"Hey!" said Bob.

"Wow," said Pete.

Jupiter, being Jupiter, reacted in a way the woman could not ignore. He bowed and said, "It's a cymbidium, isn't it?"

The woman glowed. "You know orchids! Isn't it fine? Are you a grower?"

"My uncle Egbert is," said Jupe. He lied with his customary assurance, and the woman believed him.

"I'm going to leave this at my daughter's apartment for the afternoon," said the woman, "while I take care of some chores. I'll show it tonight. I think that at last I'll get a prize."

"I wondered," said Jupiter. "Is there an orchid show in town?"

"Not a show exactly," said the woman, "just the regular monthly meeting of our local group. Sir Clive Stilton is going to speak. He's such an authority. Why don't you come? There's always a plant table, and we raffle off plants. You could bring an orchid home to your uncle. Do you live in New York?"

"No," said Jupiter. "California."

The woman handed her orchid to Pete so that she could open her purse. She took a card out and wrote an address on it. "At eight o'clock at the Statler Royal," she said. "Drop by. Your uncle would be interested to know that you saw Sir Clive. One of our members will tape his talk, and you can order a tape if you're interested."

She took back her plant and went on down the street.

Jupe looked at the card. She was Helen Innes McAuliffe, with an address in Riverdale, New York. The Statler Royal was on Seventh Avenue in the Thirties.

"Has it occurred to you that if the meeting of this orchid group was announced in the papers, Snabel might have seen the announcement?" said Jupe.

"It occurred to me about the time you started talking to the lady," said Bob. "You think Snabel might still be in New York? And would he bother to go to an orchid meeting? He's trying to keep out of sight, remember?"

"Who can tell," said Jupe. "If he's still here he has to do something with his time, and Mr. Peck says orchids are the only things he cares about."

"It's a chance," said Pete. "He might go. And what have we got to lose?"

The boys briefly discussed the advisability of asking Mr. Peck to accompany them to the orchid lecture. Pete was against it. "Temper tantrums have got to be bad for his blood pressure," said Pete, "and if Snabel is at that lecture, Grandpa will have the greatest tantrum of his career."

"What if we go and he finds out afterward?" said Bob.

Pete winced.

Still undecided about what to do, the boys went back to their hotel. There was a message for them at the desk. Mr. Peck would be detained until late that evening. The boys were to have dinner without him, and go to a movie if they liked.

That evening the boys happily had dinner at a local restaurant near their hotel reputed to have the biggest and best hero sandwiches in New York. Even Jupiter felt stuffed to the gills when they finished. They took a crosstown bus to the Statler Royal and rode up in the elevator to the grand ballroom, which was on the twelfth floor.

The grand ballroom was not really so grand. The hotel was old, and there were bare spots on the red carpeting and dust on the crystal chandeliers. When the boys got off the elevator they were greeted by a chubby man who wore a white shirt of a vaguely Oriental style. He had a name tag pinned to the shirt, so the boys knew he was Walter Bradford from Syosset. He was delighted that the boys were interested in orchids, and he was sure that Jupiter could obtain a tape of Sir Clive's talk for Jupe's mythical Uncle Egbert.

"Sir Clive will discuss breeding," said Mr. Bradford. "The importance of choosing the proper parents. It should be terribly interesting."

Pete and Bob exchanged skeptical looks.

Mr. Bradford excused himself and hurried off to greet some new arrivals. The Investigators set about exploring the layout of the twelfth floor.

The grand ballroom took up most of the floor. The corridor outside its entrance held two elevators for the hotel guests. Next to the elevator shafts there was an exit door that opened onto a stairwell. The rest rooms were down a hallway to the right, and a service elevator was down a hallway to the left. Beyond the service elevator was a small pantry. A door across the hall from the pantry led to the ballroom, and at the end of the hall was a heavy door that appeared to be a second exit to a staircase. It was not an exit, however. When Pete opened this door and peeked out, he saw only a narrow ledge protected by a guard rail and beyond that, the outdoors. There was no way off the ledge except through the door he was holding open. Pete satisfied himself about this, and then drew back into the building. The heavy door swung shut and the spring lock snapped into place.

Satisfied that Snabel would have to use either an elevator or the staircase off the main corridor if he showed up and then tried to get away from them, the boys entered the ballroom. Mr. Bradford of Syosset was now at the speaker's table. He was rapping for the group to take seats and come to order.

Orchid enthusiasts had been milling about on the outer edges of the room, where orchids were displayed on trestle tables. After Mr. Bradford had rapped for some time they drifted away from the orchids and took seats in the little gilt chairs that had been set out in rows. The dim lights in the ceiling became dimmer, and a spotlight was suddenly beamed at the speaker's table.

Mr. Bradford said a few words of greeting and then briskly got on with the purpose of the meeting, introducing the distinguished guest, Sir Clive Stilton. "Sir Clive will show slides of his orchids," said Mr. Bradford, "and he will discuss the importance of breeding from sturdy parents to obtain fine hybrids."

"Oh, boy," Pete groaned, "I'm going to have a rough time staying awake through this!"

The woman in the row in front of Pete turned and hissed at him.

He slouched low in his chair and watched as a very thin, very pink-faced man came to the speaker's table, rubbing his bony hands together, and said, "Well, now!"

The man then said nothing for a moment or two. He only beamed at the orchid enthusiasts.

Then he said, "Mr. Bradford told me a few minutes ago that he was glad to have a wet grower speaking this evening. The last speaker was a dry grower. Actually, I'm not sure I'm all that wet."

Pete began to shake with silent laughter.

Bob poked him with an elbow.

Jupe looked straight ahead and fought to keep his face straight.

Behind the Investigators, a door squeaked. Jupe turned.

"If someone will turn out the lights please?" said the speaker.

Mr. Bradford leaped to do so, and the room was black for a moment. Then a slide projector hummed into action, and on a screen was a photograph of the speaker in his greenhouse. He was hovering over a table loaded with plants.

"Now, how can we choose the best parents for our orchids? Well, the blooms are one way to tell, if you're cultivating for blooms. And isn't that what most people care about?" asked Sir Clive.

One of the doors to the corridor outside opened. Outlined in the shaft of light was a stocky figure, someone who was possibly waiting to get used to the dark.

The man at the speaker's table rattled on about flasks and seedlings and plants that would not breed true, and about how long it took for an orchid grower to see results.

The figure in the doorway moved into the dark ballroom. The door closed.

Jupe poked Pete. Then he got up and groped toward the back of the room. Pete and Bob came after him.

"I think that was Snabel who just came in," Jupe whispered. "I'm going to try to call Mr. Anderson."

He slipped out, trying not to open the door too far. Bob and Pete came after him, and for a moment they stood silent, looking around the corridor for a phone booth.

Somewhere nearby a door opened.

It was not the big door between the corridor and the ballroom. It was another door—the one down the hall near the pantry.

Was it Snabel? Had he recognized the Three Investigators as they left the ballroom? They must have been silhouetted against the light in the corridor.

There were footsteps in the little hall to the left, and the sound of crockery rattling against crockery. Then there was a rumble and a hum, and the service elevator started laboring up from a lower floor.

The boys moved cautiously to the hall and looked toward the service elevator. They saw a man in a dark suit standing there, his back to them, carrying a tray loaded with cups held at shoulder height.

A waiter! It was a waiter taking down a tray of used cups.

"Hey, he's wearing loafers!" cried Bob.

The waiter started. His head turned slightly and they saw the side of his face.

"Would you hold it a second, Mr. Snabel?" said Bob. "I'd like to get a picture of you."

Bob had his camera. It had become almost second nature for him to carry it. He pointed it now and the shutter clicked and the flash flared.

Snabel leaped toward Bob and yelled. The tray of cups crashed to the floor.

At that moment the doors of the service elevator opened. Jupe and Pete skidded around Snabel into the elevator. Jupe flipped the emergency switch that would stop the elevator where it was. Pete hit the red button that sounded the alarm. A bell clanged loudly, and kept on clanging.

"Police!" yelled Bob. He was just outside the ballroom. "Help! Murder!"

The ballroom door opened just as Snabel lurched toward Bob, ready to throttle him.

Bob snapped another picture.

Mr. Bradford shot out into the corridor, his face twisted with rage. "Stop that racket!" he cried.

Snabel paused, confused, half-blinded by the flash.

"The cops!" shrieked Bob. "Police! Call the police."

Bob's flash attachment went off again—this time right in Snabel's face.

Snabel recoiled. He clapped his hands over his eyes for a second. Then he fled back toward the service elevator.

Jupe and Pete waited in the elevator. Snabel came at them, crashing through the broken coffee cups that littered the carpet.

Then he spied the door at the end of the corridor. He saw it in spite of the spots that flashed in front of his eyes, and it must have looked like salvation to him. He made for it, arms outstretched. "Watch out!" Pete started to call, but he was too late. Snabel wrenched open the door and strode out into the darkness.

The door closed and the lock snapped shut.

People were pouring out of the ballroom now, frightened or excited or simply curious. The orchid fanciers crowded into the corridor and peeked down the hallway.

And the alarm bell in the elevator stopped ringing.

A deafening silence fell on the crowd for an instant, and in that silence everyone heard the shout. It came from the door at the end of the hall.

"Help!" It was Snabel. He started pounding on the door. "Let me in. Open the door! Help!"

Jupe calmly turned to Mr. Bradford.

"Mr. Bradford, can you tell me where the nearest public telephone is?" asked Jupe. "I have to make a call—to the FBI."

19

Mr. Sebastian Buys Lunch

The restaurant was unbelievably elegant. The tables were covered with white linen and the windows with brocade drapes. There were fresh flowers everywhere. The carpets were so deep that they smothered every footfall. Instead of a menu there was a headwaiter who made soft-voiced suggestions about what the Three Investigators should have for lunch. A waiter in a blue tailcoat and a striped vest served the meal. The food—a shrimp dish—had been prepared with such skill that it did not resemble any shrimp the boys had ever eaten before. Also, there was not very much of it.

The boys' host, their friend Hector Sebastian from back home in California, looked around the restaurant and smiled ruefully.

"When I was a down-at-the-heels private eye, I couldn't afford to eat here," he said. "Now that I've made it as a writer of mystery stories and screenplays, I can eat anywhere I want. But why in blazes did I ever want to eat here? I'm going to need a snack before the afternoon is over."

Mr. Sebastian took a sip of mineral water and grinned. "Just the same, it's nice to have money, and don't let anybody tell you different.

"Now what about your case? I called your aunt Mathilda, Jupe, when the story of Edgar Snabel broke in the papers. She was quite bewildered. She said you were supposed to be on a vacation trip with Pete's grandfather. She couldn't imagine why you were chasing spies—and what you were doing at the meeting of an orchid society."

Pete grinned. "We *are* on vacation," he said, "but we're on a case too, for my mom."

He then told how Mrs. Crenshaw had commissioned them to keep Mr. Peck out of trouble. "We did it—sort of," said Pete. "And we did some other dynamite stuff too."

"So I hear," said Mr. Sebastian. "I'm glad I happened to be in New York at the same time as you. I came to deliver my new book to Bateman, Watts. They're the publishers who brought out my last book, *Chill Factors*. My agent says they were dying to get their hands on this one. It's called . . . *Dead Silence.*"

"That's the title?" said Jupiter. "*Dead Silence?* Sounds good. What's it about?"

"You'll get a copy as soon as it's off the press," said Mr. Sebastian. "Right now I want to hear about *your* case. Are you going to write it up the way you usually do?"

"I've been working on my notes," said Bob. "We were glad when you called the hotel this morning. We wanted to know if you'd write an introduction for us."

"You bet your life I will," said Mr. Sebastian. "Fill me in on some of the details."

The boys did, starting with the first encounter with Snabel at Pismo Beach and ending with a jubilant recital of the events at the Statler Royal.

"Great!" said Mr. Sebastian. "And very professional of you to realize that a waiter in the hotel would not be wearing casual shoes like loafers. But one thing surprises me. How did you miss seeing the device on the gas tank when you looked under the car in Santa Rosa? I should think you'd have spotted it right away."

"I guess I goofed," said Jupe. "It was in the middle of the night and our flashlight batteries were dead. In all the excitement that followed, I forgot to check again. And at that point we weren't paying much attention to Mr. Peck's claims that Snabel was a sneak and a spy—which he certainly was."

"We'll never know everything about his crime. It was classified information, so the FBI told us very little. But we did learn from Mr. Anderson that Snabel had a security clearance at the plant where he worked. He was an electronics engineer, and his company made aircraft equipment. Snabel was fired from his job because he couldn't get along with any of the other technicians who worked with him. He may have turned to spying because he felt he'd been unjustly treated. He took the photographs before he left the job, and smuggled the camera out."

"He didn't have the equipment to develop his own photos and he didn't want to risk taking them to a photo shop, so he was going to turn the camera over to Bartlett. But then the cameras were switched. On top of that Mr. Peck kept on raving about how Snabel sneaked and spied. Snabel had such a guilty conscience that he thought Mr. Peck knew more than he really did."

"I love it!" cried Mr. Sebastian. "Snabel did himself in!"

Pete nodded happily. "Grandpa helped. And the farther we got on our trip, the more desperate Snabel got. He had to get that film back from Bob before Bob realized what he was carrying around and went to the authorities. The Lincoln he followed us in was Bartlett's car—or at least the one Bartlett rented so he could meet Snabel in Monterey."

"And what happened to the so-called Bartlett?" asked Mr. Sebastian.

The faces of the Three Investigators fell.

"It seems he got clean away," Jupe admitted. "Mr. Anderson told us the man had been sighted in Vienna the day after Snabel was arrested. He slipped right through the FBI net."

"Not surprising—he was obviously an experienced spy," observed Mr. Sebastian.

"Anyway, it's not as bad as it sounds," Pete put in. "I mean, the guy is going to turn over that dummy film to somebody, and when the pictures turn out to be fake, he's really going to have egg on his face! So at least we helped slow the guy down a bit."

Mr. Sebastian nodded appreciatively. "And what about your grandfather, Pete? Did he sell his invention?"

Pete beamed. "He did. He really struck it rich this time. I mean, not in money maybe, but this idea really works and it's practical."

"We couldn't find it anywhere in the car because it wasn't in the car. Grandpa had mailed it to the

Riverview Plaza, where we stayed when we first got here, and he'd asked them to hold it until he arrived. It was in the hotel safe the whole time. That's why he wasn't really frantic when he thought Snabel was trying to get it—he was just furious."

"But what is the invention?" said Mr. Sebastian. "Why was it so hush-hush?"

"Because it *is* kind of a military secret," said Pete. "Well, not really military, but important to our space program. It's a new kind of valve that Grandpa figured out while he was working on a sprinkler system for the church hall. It's got an automatic sensor in it, and it's smaller than the valves they're using now and more efficient. It can regulate the temperature and pressure in a spacesuit so that the suit doesn't have to be so bulky. Less insulation is needed. So astronauts can have more freedon if they have to leave their ships."

"So he really had something!" exclaimed Mr. Sebastian.

"Right. Now Grandpa is having lots of meetings with some firm that's one of the main suppliers for NASA. He's got a lawyer, and agreements are being worked out. Actually it's sort of a bummer that he's been so busy lately. He can sometimes drive you crazy with his temper, but mostly he's fun to be around."

"He's certainly full of beans," said Mr. Sebastian.

"It sounds as if you and your grandfather have really gotten to know each other on this trip."

Pete smiled in agreement.

"Now, boys," said Mr. Sebastian, "if Mr. Peck will give you the afternoon off, I have something that might interest you: tickets to a Broadway play, *Deathtrap*! It's full of mystery and intrigue."

"That sounds great," Jupiter said.

Pete and Bob nodded excitedly.

"It's a matinee," said Mr. Sebastian, "so we'd better get moving."

"There's just one thing, Mr. Sebastian," Jupiter added.

"Yes, Jupe," said the mystery writer.

"Could we possibly pick up a snack along the way?"

The Three Investigators Mystery Series